ONCE UPON A SUMMER

ONCE UPON A
SUMMER

Julie Coffin

CHIVERS

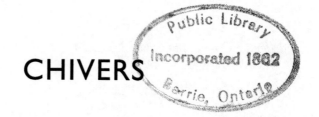

British Library Cataloguing in Publication Data available

This Large Print edition published by AudioGO Ltd, Bath, 2011.
Published by arrangement with the Author.

U.K. Hardcover ISBN 978 1 408 49343 4
U.K. Softcover ISBN 978 1 408 49344 1

Printed and bound in Great Britain by
CPI Antony Rowe, Chippenham and Eastbourne

CHAPTER ONE

Tom barked in his usual abrupt way. 'I want a harbour. Cornwall. Small, unspoilt.' His steely gaze speared into me. 'So, Lissa, don't make it a marina full of luxury yachts, will you?' He flicked through the typescript scattering the desk. 'And cliffs. Always looks good to have a few raging waves crashing over jagged rocks, creating lots of spray. Dramatic. Atmospheric. Remember that, Lissa. Cliffs.'

You've probably guessed by now that my job was finding suitable locations for television drama series. You know the kind of thing. That pretty Miss Marple-type village with ivy-covered cottages and flower-filled gardens, although I must confess that we sometimes cheated on those a little. It's amazing how a few carefully placed pots of different plants can turn autumn into spring. Or that Jane Austen-style of stately home with a curving gravelled driveway for the carriages to sweep along, past fields full of grazing sheep.

I travelled the country, and sometimes abroad, looking for just the right place for all the locations we needed.

I really don't know why I continued working for a man like Tom though, especially after what had happened. He treated all his staff as if we were morons. But it was a well-paid job and those weren't too easy to find with a recession and cut-backs everywhere. And I loved doing that kind of work. Every day was a challenge.

For the next two weeks I toured miles of desolate coastline. January is one of the bleakest months, so you can imagine what it was like. I can't believe just how many Cornish harbours there are. Some merely a cleft in the cliff with a cluster of fishing boats hauled up by chains. Others, curved like a horse-shoe, surrounded by granite walls.

Each day I emailed a dozen or more photographs back to Tom. None met with his approval.

'I know exactly what I want, Lissa, and so should you.' His sharp comments scorched out of my mobile. 'For goodness' sake get a move on. Filming starts next month. Just hurry up and find it.'

And then, quite by coincidence, I did.

Fine rain was misting the windscreen as I drove along yet another narrow winding lane, with arching trees overhead. Puddles stretched across from side to side, hiding deep potholes. It was late afternoon, growing dark. I was hungry, tired and fed up. If Tom was going to be this fussy, he could come down and do the search himself.

The road twisted sharply, first one way, then the other until, as I rounded the final bend, I saw white plumes of spray rising high above a low sea wall, and the masts of three tall ships. Braking, I pulled the car into the side of the road and stared in disbelief.

Narrow harbour. Old ships. A raging sea. And cliffs. This had to be what Tom wanted. Tugging out my digital camera, I began to photograph.

Through the skeins of misty drizzle blowing in from the sea, a swaying sign showing a three-masted boat in full sail creaked above a grey granite building. I went inside to ask about accommodation for the night.

'Rooms are available,' the barmaid said slowly. 'Not at this time of year though. Easter's when our season begins.'

'But it's only for tonight,' I pleaded in desperation.

She shook her head. 'I'm sorry, my dear. No staff in the winter months, you see. There's only me and I've enough to do, running the bar and cooking meals. Gets busy here in the evenings. Only pub in the village, you see. But my husband's home from his work over at the Eden Project by then, to help out.'

'Is there anywhere else nearby? Just a B&B would do.'

Pursing her mouth, she thought for a moment, before shaking her head again. 'Bit bleak round here at this time as you can see, so nowhere stays open. A few visitors do come down for Christmas or New Year, but after that there's nobody. Can I get you some soup or coffee to warm you? You look as if you need it.'

'Some soup would be lovely,' I said.

'Nice pan of cauliflower and stilton, I've made. My husband enjoys a bowl when he comes in. Gets chilly, working outdoors, over at Eden. It's a favourite for my customers, too. Would that be all right for you?'

'Sounds delicious. Thank you.'

At least I wouldn't be hungry, even if I did have to sleep in the car that night, I decided, sinking wearily onto a leather bench by the window, overlooking the sea. Rain was lashing down now, widening the large puddles already filling the lane. A ferocious wind whipped waves high into the air, sending them swirling in through the narrow entrance between the granite walls of the harbour.

Wiping some of the condensation from the glass, I took a few more photos of the scene to send to Tom. If those didn't interest him, I thought, nothing would.

'There, my dear. This should fill you up a bit.'

A steaming earthenware bowl was placed in front of me, with a hunk of crusty bread and little pot of butter, and I sighed in anticipation.

'How about a nice slice of apple pie for afterwards? I've one just out of the oven. With some clotted cream?' the woman said, smiling down at me.

'That would be fantastic!'

I was just licking the last specks of cream from my spoon when the door behind me suddenly crashed open, letting in a flurry of wind and rain, and I turned my head to look at the man who'd entered. Not that I could see much of him, muffled as he was in a dripping wet Barbour jacket with the collar turned up. His hair clung close to his head, dark with rain, hiding its true colour.

'Ah, now here's a person who might be able to help you, my dear,' the woman said, her plump face creasing into a broad smile as she moved out from the bar to speak to him.

I saw his eyes study me for a moment, and he hesitated before coming over to where I sat by the window.

'Mags says you're looking for somewhere to stay?' His voice held the deep burr of the West Country.

'Just for tonight,' I said.

A raindrop meandered slowly down his tanned cheek and I watched it, fascinated, until it reached the cleft of his chin and was lost.

He frowned slightly, sending deep lines across into the dampness of his hair and I noticed his eyes were a grey-blue, under surprisingly thick lashes.

'I'm afraid we're not actually open to the public yet,' he said slowly, and I felt my shoulders droop with disappointment, as he continued. 'You see, the house is still being

5

refurbished over the winter before the season.'

I raised my eyes to gaze pleadingly back into the blue depths of his and saw the sympathy that filled them.

'But,' he added quickly. 'If you really don't mind putting up with a lot of chaos, I'm sure we'll be able to find you a room. Do you want a lift, or have you a car with you?'

'A car,' I murmured, almost too exhausted to reply.

'Give me a couple of minutes to bring in some cauliflowers for Mags, then I'll show you the way. It's a bit off the beaten track.'

*   *   *

Off the beaten track was an understatement. The lane became even narrower, as I followed his battered and mud-caked old Range Rover. Every few metres there were potholes, deep with water that thudded against the underside of my car, until I was terrified a wheel would come off.

Eventually, the Range Rover turned in through two stone gateposts, yellow with lichen, and up a long gravelled drive-way, bordered by dripping dark-leaved rhododendron bushes. And then, unexpectedly, the drive opened out into a wide circle in front of the pillared entrance to a large and ancient house.

I'd been expecting a country cottage or

maybe even a farmhouse, but not what looked to me like a very dilapidated stately home.

'You can leave your car here,' he said, leaning his wet head in through the window as I opened it. 'I'll put it into one of the stables once this weather eases off a little. Come on, we'd better run inside quickly before you get drenched.'

Bent against the driving rain, I followed him through an arched wooden door that opened into a square courtyard. Another door on the far side, led into the chill of a stone-floored hall.

'This is the only wing of the house we're able to use at the moment while building is going on,' he explained, tugging off his Barbour jacket and hanging it on a hook among years of old coats. Smiling, he caught hold of my elbow, guiding me down a narrow corridor. 'Don't look so worried, I promise you it'll be warmer in here.'

The room we entered was huge. Mullioned windows, hung with well-worn red velvet curtains; a polished wooden floor with a faded but once beautiful, square carpet; huge velvet and chintz covered armchairs and sofas that were almost lost in the spaciousness; and a crackling fire of enormous blazing logs.

With hands outstretched, I moved quickly towards it.

'Introduce me, Daniel.'

The voice startled me. I hadn't noticed the

7

elderly lady, wrapped in a pale pink mohair shawl, who was curled up in one of the armchairs by the fire.

'Gran, this is . . .' He hesitated, and raised one eyebrow at me. 'I'm sorry, but I've no idea of your name.'

'Melissa Thornton,' I said, and felt like curtseying before this regal old lady with her compelling manner. 'But everybody calls me Lissa.'

'I'm Olivia Tregenna, Miss Thornton.' A thin, heavily veined hand reached out from the depths of the chair and I took it gently, frightened it would crumble in mine.

'Well, where are your manners Daniel? I'm sure Miss Thornton would like some tea.' Her faded blue eyes scanned over me. 'She looks somewhat wet to me.'

'I'll just go and find Mrs Tolly, and have a room made up, Gran. Melissa is staying here overnight.'

'Tea first, Daniel. Earl Grey, I think.' The old lady's voice was quite firm. 'We shall drink it while Miss Thornton and I become acquainted. Now, my dear, do sit down by the fire and get warm. You look extremely chilled.'

A log settled in the huge open grate, sending up a shower of sparks that glowed scarlet before vanishing among the embers and the smell of wood-smoke, mingled with pine resin, drifted warmly round me as I sank into one of the deep armchairs.

'Now, Miss Thornton, kindly tell me why we have the pleasure of your company here. Daniel didn't mention we were to have visitors.'

Pulling the chair a little closer to hers, I began to explain.

'A television series about Cornwall? Historical, you say. Now that I find very interesting.' Mrs Tregenna slipped a small embroidered cushion behind her back, gathered the shawl more closely round her shoulders, and sat upright. 'Daniel must show you some of our family documents. We were mine-owners, you see. Copper and tin. Once very prosperous. That's how this house was built.' She sighed. 'Sadly all the mines are now gone. So much cheaper to import from abroad. But in those days . . .'

'Not so good if you were a miner though, Gran,' Daniel said, coming into the room carrying a large tray. 'Spending your whole life—and a pitifully brief one at that—miles underground, in horrendous conditions. A candle stuck on your hat. Walls dripping with water. All for a pittance.'

He poured tea from an ornate silver pot into thin china cups.

'Well, my boy, you wouldn't be living in this house if it wasn't for them,' Mrs Tregenna replied sharply, as he placed one cup on a small table beside her and spooned in two lots of sugar.

9

'No, Gran, I realise that,' he said, passing another cup to me. 'And it doesn't make me any happier to know the suffering it was built from.'

'But this is quite amazing,' I said, hardly able to believe my luck. 'That's what the new TV series is about. Tin and copper mining. It's based on the lives of two Cornish families— one, a mine-owner and the other, a miner.'

I was surprised to see that Daniel's jaw had tightened significantly.

'Then you've certainly come to the right place for that,' he said grimly.

'As you will observe, Miss Thornton,' Mrs Tregenna said rather crossly, 'My grandson has a very strange guilt complex about his heritage, but for now we shall forget all about that and enjoy our tea, while Daniel advises Mrs Tolly on which bedroom is suitable for you.' She waved her hand towards a plate. 'Please help yourself to a cucumber sandwich, my dear. Mrs Tolly always produces excellent ones.'

Later, Daniel led me up a wide staircase that climbed from the hallway, turning twice before it reached the floor above. My room, when we entered it, was square and quite plain, with a high ceiling and newly painted white walls. The polished wooden floor had a scattering of rather threadbare rugs. But the centrepiece was a fantastic four-poster bed, hung with red brocaded cloth. A bed for a

10

princess—or a honeymoon.

'This doesn't seem like the usual B&B,' I said, turning to look at him.

He laughed. 'That's because it's not.'

'What is it, then?'

'As I told you at the pub, the house is being refurbished. The intention was to run it as a country house hotel, but you can see just how dilapidated the whole place has become over the years. Every room the builders start work on is in a much worse condition than they anticipated. And it's costing far more than we ever estimated.'

His long fingers raked through his thick shaggy hair and I saw that, now it had dried, it was a tawny shade, like warm sand on a summer's day.

'This one wing of the house is the only part we've been able to complete, so you're our first—and probably only—guest. Officially, the season beings at Easter.' He sighed. 'Although I doubt it'll ever be finished by then, if at all. Since we started the venture over a year ago, the recession has hit us badly. The money just isn't there any more. My grandmother doesn't understand that, though. She's always been used to living to a high standard.'

His grey-blue eyes were clouded with worry when he looked at me. 'I hope I haven't conned you into coming here, Lissa, but Mags did say you were rather desperate for somewhere to stay, and you looked so very sad and weary sitting there. I couldn't just abandon you, could I?'

His anxious expression deepened. 'Look, whatever Mags would have charged, we'll do the same. Or maybe a little less, as it's all a bit—well, very—chaotic still.'

I smiled. 'Don't look so worried, Daniel. Charge whatever is the going rate. The TV company pays all my expenses—and I'm sure that, once Tom knows about it, he'll be keen for me to delve into your family's mining history. And anyway, it is only for one night.'

To my delight, the photos I'd emailed on my laptop to Tom that evening were approved when he phoned me.

'What's the name of this place, Lissa? Email directions straight away. I'll be there midday tomorrow.'

Tom never wasted time. He always knew exactly what he wanted. Once it had been me. Not any more though. That part of my life was over. And I was quite sure he at least had completely forgotten it. For him, what was there to remember?

By ten o'clock I was really exhausted and ready for bed. Dinner had been a formal affair. With Daniel's grandmother, now dressed in black velvet and wearing a pearl necklace, it couldn't be anything else.

Red candles. Silver cutlery. Beautiful china. Crystal glasses. Wine. The fish for the main course was fresh from the sea that morning,

Daniel told me. While the peaches in brandy had been grown in their own garden glasshouses. As for the clotted cream, that was another local produce, and so was the delicious cheese.

From my bedroom window, I could see and hear the sea. All night it thundered against the cliffs, and the beam of a lighthouse flashed rhythmically, sending shadows around the room. Tired though I was, it made it impossible to sleep. I found myself counting the seconds until the light came again, so it must have been around 2am before I eventually managed to doze off.

A sound. A rustle of movement, maybe. I don't really know what, but it woke me. And then I saw the child. How, I'm not sure, as the room was dark, and yet I knew it was there.

Whether a boy or girl, I couldn't tell, or even what it was wearing. But its eyes were wide in a small round face and it just stood, or maybe sat, silently, gazing at me, near the end of my bed.

CHAPTER TWO

The beam of the lighthouse blazed in again, illuminating every corner of the the whole bedroom, but the child was gone. Nothing strange about that, I decided drowsily. Mrs

Tolly, the housekeeper, obviously had a child. Being curious about a stranger staying there, it had crept in to peep. Children were like that. Full of curiosity. Pulling the folds of the blankets round me, I slid back into sleep.

It was only in the morning, when bright sunshine flooded in through the heavy velvet curtains to wake me, that I thought any more about it. And remembered my bedroom door was locked from the inside, something I did automatically, after what had happened all those years before.

I needed to ask Daniel. But when I went down for breakfast, his grandmother told me he'd already eaten and gone out.

'At this time of year it's broccoli, cauliflowers, daffodils and narcissi to pick and deliver, then later, in a month or so, it will be new potatoes,' she said. 'Daniel has had to put all the fields on the estate to use. He worries so much about money, I'm afraid. Now there is always something growing throughout the year.' She took a slice of thin toast from the rack and carefully buttered it. 'You see, my dear, we have the advantage of a very mild climate down here for our early produce.' The network of lines across her forehead deepened as she frowned. 'But those vicious gales in mid-December gave the narcissi that were ready for the Christmas trade rather a blasting. Quite a set-back, that was, for poor Daniel.'

Spooning marmalade from a glass dish, she

spread it on the toast. 'Unfortunately, nowadays it's so difficult to find workers. I suppose, in a way, you can't blame them. Who wants to spend back-breaking hours in a muddy field, cutting vegetables or flowers with freezing fingers and rain trickling down your neck? Much easier to earn a small fortune, sitting all day in front of one of those computing things, ruining your eyesight and growing ever more obese. More coffee, my dear?' Picking up the percolator, she refilled our cups.

'We do have a small band of stalwarts, the Polruans, who've been with us for years. But Daniel is out there for most of the daylight hours, in between chasing up builders or surveyors or whatever. He's determined to keep this house in the family, whatever it takes, but I'm beginning to fear he's fighting a losing battle, although I daren't tell him that.'

'Well I'd better go to say goodbye and thank him,' I said, brushing toast crumbs from my jeans. 'And settle my bill.'

'Bill?' Mrs Tregenna raised finely arched eyebrows. 'What are you talking about, my dear? You are our guest. Please don't insult us by talking about a bill.' Her thin hand shook slightly, rattling the cup as she replaced it on the saucer.

'You will find some wellingtons under the coats in the hall. You appear to have quite small feet, so mine will most probably fit you.

It's inches deep in mud out there, after all this rain.'

Pointing through the window, she gave me directions. 'Over that stile in the far wall, through the orchard, then follow the path on the south side. You will hear the tractor somewhere around. That will be Daniel. It's so old and temperamental that he won't let anyone else take the risk of driving it.'

*   *   *

After all the rain and strong wind of the previous day, long wisps of cloud hid the sun, but when it managed to break through it was surprisingly warm. I undid the buttons on my suede jacket as I skirted the edge of a field where three ponies nibbled grass under a tree, raising their heads in curiosity, then went back to the grass, ignoring me.

Just as Mrs Tregenna had suggested, I heard the tractor before I saw it, bumping along the rutted path, hauling a trailer piled with cauliflowers. Daniel raised one muddy hand and waved, his mouth curving into a wide smile of welcome, and I waited until he was alongside.

'If you're going for a walk, I wouldn't advise this track. There are some huge puddles further along. Hop up and I'll give you a lift back to the house,' he said, his fingers curling round mine as he tugged me up beside him into the cab.

Travelling along the track on the tractor made the pot-holey lanes seem like a motorway, as we jerked and swayed over every lump and rut.

'I came to say goodbye,' I shouted above the noise of the engine. 'You're probably too busy at the moment to give me my bill, but I'll authorise the company to settle it, if you send it on to me.'

'Sorry?' he said, cupping his hand round one ear and leaning sideways, his shoulder brushing mine. 'You'll have to say that again once I've switched this thing off.'

In the sunshine his hair was quite fair, standing up like a halo above the deeply tanned skin of his forehead and reaching thickly down the back of his neck. Mud smeared his cheek and the collar of his blue check shirt was tucked in at one side, under the frayed edge of his sweatshirt.

Resisting the impulse to untuck it, I felt my breath catch in my throat as my heartbeat quickened.

There was a sudden silence as the engine cut out and I heard my voice waver slightly as I repeated the words. Briefly, I was aware of the change of expression in Daniel's grey-blue eyes.

Could it be disappointment? Whatever it was, it was gone in a flash. 'Goodbye then, Melissa,' he said quietly.

17

His hand was warm as it gripped mine for one long moment, while I climbed down, his fingers slowly slipping away from mine. Then, the tractor roared into life again and regretfully I watched it, and Daniel, jolt away from me down the track. When it reached the open gate into the field, I hoped he might tum and wave, but it disappeared round the corner, and he was gone.

As I crossed the garden to the house, I could hear a raised voice. A voice I recognised only too well.

'Where the blue blazes is she?'

It was Tom. Hurrying across to the driveway in front of the house, I went over to meet him.

'I told you I'd be here at midday, Lissa. Why weren't you waiting? You know I hate wasting valuable time.' He flung open the car door. 'Well, come on, hop to it, get in.'

Before I could even do up the seatbelt, and with a spatter of gravel as he swung the steering wheel, the car was moving smoothly down the drive and into the lane. Even the pot-holes seemed non-existent.

'I see you've located a suitable house.'

'House?' I repeated, finally managing to click the buckle into place. 'Harbour, you mean.'

'Lissa,' he rapped out impatiently. 'When I say house, I mean house. That one back there. Excellent. You've made all the arrangements, I take it?'

'Arrangements? Well no, I didn't realise you wanted me to.'

'Lissa,' he cut in. 'What are you paid a ridiculous salary to do?'

His profile was clear-cut and strikingly handsome. His gaze not leaving the road ahead as we swung round each bend with terrifying speed. I knew every inch of that face. Every expression. Every mood.

'Well, the answer to that is only too easy. It's to anticipate exactly what I want, Lissa. You should know that by now. You've been with me long enough, haven't you?'

Yes, I thought bitterly. Too long. And yet I stayed. But why? It wasn't because I loved him any more. That love was killed long ago, at the time when everything happened.

White gulls hovered against the blue sky as we reached the harbour. Every tiny wave glinted in the sunshine. Shadows dappled the grey stones of the seawall, and the inn sign swayed gently to and fro, creaking.

Tom stopped the car and stepped out.

Tensely biting my lower lip, I waited for his reaction.

'Not bad. Not bad at all.'

My taut body relaxed a little. From Tom that was praise indeed. 'Right, Lissa. We'll be taking over the house back there for the duration of the series. Sort it all out, will you. Shooting begins in ten days.'

He waved a leather-gloved hand in the air.

19

'Get a crew down here to eliminate all this modern stuff cluttering up the area round the harbour—TV aerials, yellow lines, road signs, lamp-posts, whatever. You know the procedure, Lissa. Keep me posted. ' 'Bye.'

I stood watching his car glide away. It was typical of Tom. He gave orders, not requests and took it for granted that what he said would be carried out without any question, or failure, leaving me to make sure.

Why I didn't leave, I'll never know.

With Tom's car disappearing round the bend of the hill, leaving me stranded, I had to get back to the house. And once I got back there, I needed to find Daniel and put Tom's request to him. Climbing the steep stone steps into the Ship Inn, I went to find Mags to ask her about a taxi.

*   *   *

'Stay on? Of course, Lissa. No problem,' Daniel replied, when I eventually discovered him bunching tight buds of daffodils and narcissi with elastic bands at a long bench in one of the old stables.

'There is something else,' I said hesitantly, smoothing a fallen flower with my fingers. 'What would you say about the house being used in our television production?'

Still mentally counting the stems as he bunched them, Daniel's startled eyes glanced

20

up at me. 'Used?'

'Tom wants to film, inside and out. Your grandmother did say it was originally a mine-owner's house, so it really would be authentic, and also save a lot of time and money building sets in the studio,' I gabbled. 'I'd make quite sure there wasn't too much disruption. And the company does pay extremely well for this sort of thing.'

Daniel closed the lid on a flower-filled box.

'What sort of disruption?' he asked quietly. 'Be honest, Lissa. I don't mind for myself, but there's my grandmother to consider. She's already had to put up with all the refurbishing so far.'

'It's impossible not to create some upheaval,' I admitted. 'And the crew do rather take over, I'm afraid. Could I have a look at the rest of the house? You said you only live in one wing, but not the others. Maybe some of the un-lived-in areas could be used.'

'Give me an hour to finish bunching these and I'll take you on a conducted tour.'

'Don't you have anyone to help you?' I asked, eyeing the enormous heap of flowers.

'Matty Polruan and his wife are still out there, cutting more, so they'll be along soon.' He grinned, teasingly at me. 'It takes a bit of practise, but you can try if you like. Ten to a bunch and the elastic band is twisted twice, just here. Like this.' His long fingers guided mine, and maybe it was my imagination or just

21

wishful thinking, but I thought they lingered, holding mine for a fraction of a second after the flowers were secured.

While I completed one bunch, Daniel did at least a dozen, his hands moving rapidly in a kind of rhythm. But once the Polruans had joined us and we'd filled the final box, we washed the sticky sap from our fingers and were ready to explore the uninhabited wings of the old house.

'Through here,' Daniel said, unlocking a heavy wooden door on the opposite side of the courtyard.

It led into a huge tiled hallway, where the once-white plaster on the walls was stained with patches of damp, and falling away. The only light came in through grimy windows, some with coloured glass round the edges, cracked in places, and a glass dome high above.

'Watch out as you go up the stairs,' Daniel warned. 'Some of these treads are a bit fragile and sections of the banisters are missing.'

Cautiously, I began to climb. Once upon a time, the staircase had been beautiful, curving upwards, but the view from the top all the way down into the black and white tiled hallway was scary, knowing just how hazardous the banisters might be if I leaned over to look.

'You need to keep close to the wall as you walk along this corridor,' Daniel said, catching hold of my elbow to move me sideways. 'A few of the floorboards in the middle could give way.'

Through open doors I could see into empty rooms where the ceilings bulged and paper hung in strips from the walls. There was a throat-catching smell of mustiness and damp. Black mould crept along skirting boards and clinging cobwebs drifted across our faces as we passed through them.

'This wing of the house hasn't been used for years,' Daniel murmured, frowning as he looked at the dereliction.

'But it could be made beautiful again,' I insisted.

He smiled ruefully and shook his head. 'Lissa, it would cost a fortune to renovate. Money I shall never have, I'm afraid.

'It's only the rooms on the outer side that are the worst,' I said. 'Those facing the courtyard haven't been so badly affected by the weather. It wouldn't take much to make them look respectable.'

'This was the original part of the house, Lissa. Over the years the other wings were added by those inheriting it. Unfortunately, the family fortune dwindled when the tin and copper mines began to close down. That's when the house started to become neglected.'

'Then this is the authentic part where the mine-owner lived and so it should be used for the filming. I'll authorise for the renovations to be started straight away,' I said eagerly.

'Please don't look so worried, Daniel, Tom leaves everything to me. There won't be any problem.'

'Are you and this Tom . . . what's the term . . . an item?'

'Once,' I said rather more abruptly than I'd intended. 'Not any more.'

'And yet you still work with him?'

'Yes,' I said slowly. 'I still work with him. It's called being civilised, Daniel. And, anyway, with a fantastic salary, plus all the travelling and meeting so many different people, I love my job too much to give it up.'

'You must do,' he said dryly. 'Look, it's getting far too dark to stay up here safely any longer and I have to drive those flowers to the station.' His fingers lightly held my wrist. 'Mind how you go down these stairs.'

*   *   *

That night, through my bedroom window, I could see stars studding the sky like splinters of diamond. Something not easily seen above the London streets with their bright lights. Out to sea more lights twinkled. Fishing boats, I guessed and was glad the sea was calm again for them.

The beam from the lighthouse flared out, then vanished. It had been a busy day and I was tired, so tonight I would sleep. The four-poster bed was warm and welcoming as I sank

24

down into the crisp sheets and blankets, my eyes closing.

And then, much nearer this time, the child was there again. I could see the perfect outline of its face, those wide eyes studying me, filled with such sadness. A sadness that overwhelmed me.

'Who are you?' I whispered, and yet I knew.

But even as I spoke the words, I realised the room, lit once more by the beam of the lighthouse, was empty. No one was there.

I wasn't dreaming. I couldn't be. The child was too real. And for the rest of the night I lay awake, remembering. But not wanting to remember.

CHAPTER THREE

It was still dark when I heard the creak of boards in the corridor outside. Swiftly, I ran across the room and opened the door, to see Daniel's back as he descended the stairs. His head turned, eyes wide and startled.

'Sorry, did I wake you?'

I shook my head, struggling to push my arms into the sleeves of my dressing-gown as I hurried to catch up with him.

'Is something wrong?' he asked, concerned. 'It's only 6am. You should still be asleep.'

We'd reached the kitchen now and he

switched on the light and began to fill the kettle from the tap. I perched myself on one of the high wooden stools by the table and watched him cut two thick slices of bread and drop them into the toaster.

'I want to ask you something, Daniel.'

'Ask away then.'

'Does—Mrs Tolly, I think you said her name is—does she have a child?'

'Three,' he replied, laughing as he put blue pottery mugs on the table and spooned in coffee from a large jar. 'All hefty great fishermen that she's always complaining should get married and leave home, instead of having her to wait on them hand and foot. She'd miss them though, and the fish, if they did, and so would we.'

Lifting out the toast, he handed me a slice. 'She lives down in the village with them all. Why do you ask? Help yourself to butter. All locally made.'

'I know it sounds silly, and you'll probably say I dreamed it.' I paused.

'But,' he prompted, pushing a jar of marmalade across the table.

'Both nights I've been here, I've seen a small child in my room.' He raised one eyebrow. 'I knew you wouldn't believe me,' I said crossly. 'But I'm certain I wasn't asleep and dreaming. Besides, I've seen it twice now.'

'Does this child say or do anything?'

I put my hands round the mug, warming

them, before I sipped the coffee.

'No. It just looks at me with huge, wide eyes,' I said, remembering. 'Oh, Daniel, its expression is filled with such an awful sadness. I just want to reach out and cuddle it close.'

As I spoke, tears welled up in my own eyes, and I breathed hard, blinking them away before they slid down my cheeks.

'It has to be a dream, Lissa,' he said gently. 'You do seem to have a very stressful and demanding job working with this Tom. And what with all the rushing around the country you do, you must get pretty exhausted. The mind can play funny tricks at times.'

I thumped the mug down, slopping coffee over the wooden table.

'I knew you'd say something like that. Just because . . .' But my voice trailed away.

'Just because what, Lissa?'

'It doesn't matter,' I said tersely, standing up. 'Anyway, I need to start getting everything organised.' I watched his long fingers tip a spoonful of sugar into his mug and stir it. 'You are quite sure you're happy about us using the old wing of the house, aren't you? If you're really certain, we can discuss a fee and I'll arrange for a contract to be drawn up for you to sign.' I took a bite of toast and crunched it. 'Are there any contractors around here that you'd like us to employ for the renovation? Local labour would make it a lot quicker, and easier.'

27

'Anything that brings work into this area is always very welcome by me, Lissa. I'll give you a list of names. Trade is a bit slack at this time of year, and the recession hasn't helped, so there shouldn't be any problem finding the right craftsmen to begin straight away.'

Finishing the toast, I licked a scrap of marmalade from my thumb. 'Look, Daniel, I know you're busy, but can you make that list now? The sooner I contact them, the quicker they can get going. Filming starts in ten days, so there's not a great deal of time.'

Daniel swallowed the dregs of his coffee and went out into the hall, returning with a copy of Yellow Pages in his hand. Sifting back down at the table, he began to flip through until he found the right section, and started underlining names and telephone numbers.

'Try those,' he said, passing the book across to me. 'They're all men I've known for years and can personally vouch for their work.'

*　　　*　　　*

The rest of the day was spent going through the list, using my mobile phone, and emailing the London office. Tom, as so frequently happened, was out of the department, and I wondered which of his latest 'interests' he was with. If so, I knew from experience that his mobile would be switched off for hours.

In a way I was glad as that meant I could go

ahead and finalise all the arrangements, before he had a chance to veto anything—especially as I knew the large fee I'd offered Daniel before I drew up the contract wouldn't please him at all.

By late afternoon, as the sun disappeared below the rim of the sea, creating an aurora of scarlet, fuchsia and rose to tint the sky, I had most things under control. Too late now, I hoped, for Tom to make any changes.

I remembered his earlier stinging words. 'What are you paid a ridiculous salary to do? Well, the answer to that is only too easy. It's to anticipate exactly what I want, Lissa. You should know that by now. You've been with me long enough, haven't you?'

Well, I thought, that's exactly what I've done —and you're not going to like it one bit.

*   *   *

Daniel was alone in the bunching shed when I found him, packing boxes of flowers, ready for despatch.

'I've arranged for the contract to be sent down from London tonight by special courier. All it needs is your signature and then he can take it straight back there.'

His fingers deftly twisted an elastic band round the daffodils before he looked up at me. 'Why the rush? I thought you said filming doesn't start for another ten days.'

There was no way I could tell him the truth. That I wanted everything finalised before Tom could object to the financial details in the contract, as I felt sure he would.

'I like everything signed and settled quickly. That's how I work.'

'And this Tom of yours is in agreement, is he? It seems an awful lot of money to offer me, Lissa, especially as your TV company will be providing all that renovation.'

My hair fell round my face, hiding my expression as I leaned forward and gathered ten sterns together.

'He has agreed, Lissa, hasn't he?'

'He's been out of the office all day, so I haven't been able to contact him yet,' I said, keeping my eyes fixed on the flowers I was bunching. 'But it'll be okay, Daniel. Tom leaves everything to me and I've never known him to disagree with any arrangements I've made.'

Yet, I thought, but I've never offered anyone such a large sum of money before. Anyway, if Daniel signed the contract and I sent it back with the courier that night, it would be too late for Tom to do anything about it when he arrived the next morning.

'Have you eaten today?' Daniel asked suddenly, studying my face in the gloom of the shed.

'I had breakfast.'

'Half a slice of toast?' he said scornfully. 'No

wonder you look so pale and peaky. When I take these down to the station, you're coming with me and we'll eat out. There's a good place over at Marazion.'

'But what about your grandmother?' I asked. 'She hardly ever sees you. We can't just leave her to eat dinner on her own.'

'Gran's had some of her friends here to lunch with her and play bridge this afternoon, so she'll be quite tired. Mrs Tolly will make her a light supper, then she'll go to bed early and watch television. There's an Agatha Christie on tonight, and she loves those.'

'But,' I began.

'No buts, Lissa. Call it a celebration. It's not every day I receive an offer of money like the one you've given me.'

Why am I protesting, I thought, when I want to be with him so much?

Daniel parked the Range Rover by the sea wall at Marazion, lightly holding my elbow as we walked in darkness over the cobbles to a small hotel right by the water's edge. Inside, warmth and a pleasant hubbub of voices greeted us.

The view from the windows, across to St Michael's Mount, was spellbinding, and I wished I could capture it on film to send to Tom, but I hadn't brought my camera with me.

A full moon silhouetted the outline of the castle, situated right at the top of the island, against the clear night sky. Below it, lights

31

from a terrace of houses lining the harbour-side were reflected, like a necklace of tiny twinkling diamonds, onto the slight swell of the sea.

A perfect night. A perfect place. And perfect company. I felt my body slowly begin to unwind in the comfort of the room.

'There's a causeway leading over to the island.' Daniel's voice broke into my thoughts. 'It's only uncovered for a few hours each day, so when the tide is in little boats ferry people across to the harbour over there.'

'And then what?' I asked, breaking off a piece of thick granary bread and buttering it.

His wide mouth curved into a smile that made my heartbeat race. 'And then you climb up a very steep and rugged path to the castle, where you can see for miles on a clear day. It's beautiful. You really should go over there sometime.'

'It looks spectacular from here. Do you know if there are any mining connections, so that we could use the island in the filming? Tom likes dramatic locations and this is quite amazing.'

'All I've heard is that records show it was an important port for the trading of Cornish tin, way back in the first century, but you'll need to delve into its history to make quite certain.'

The food was simple, but delicious. Thick, homemade cauliflower and stilton soup, so popular in the area. Crisply grilled mackerel with fresh vegetables and jacket potatoes. Clove-flavoured apple crumble, smothered in rich clotted cream. And a red wine that was silkily smooth. I couldn't remember when I'd last enjoyed a meal so much.

Candles flickered on the tables, creating shadows that wrapped us in our own secluded world of enchantment. I didn't even notice if others were eating there as well. All I saw was Daniel—all I wanted to see was Daniel.

The soft candlelight outlined the shaggy tumble of his hair, growing thick and lush down the back of his neck to rest on the collar of his shirt. And I wondered whether he ever had enough time to have it cut. His nose was quite firm and straight. Possibly what people call Grecian, I decided.

So late in the day, his upper lip and jaw were faintly darkened, while the corners of his wide mouth tilted upwards at the corners. It was a mouth that revealed kindness and humour. And suddenly I wanted to know its kiss.

Slowly I raised my gaze to his eyes, and was surprised by the expression in them as they looked back into mine. Surely there was no way he could read my thoughts?

As we ate, he told me more of the history of the area, intermingled with its mystical legends, like that of the wicked giant Cormoran. How a local boy called Jack dug a deep pit halfway down the Mount at night while the giant was asleep. Then, in the morning, stood on the far side of it, blowing a horn to wake him, so that Cormoran rushed down, with the sun shining right into his eyes, and fell into it to die.

'Even now,' Daniel said, 'you can see a stone, shaped like a heart, said to be that of the giant, on the path leading up to the top of the Mount.'

He leaned across the table to fill my coffee cup, before continuing.

'And, of course, everyone knows that the island is dedicated to the Archangel St Michael, after some fishermen in the year 495 saw him standing on a ledge of rock, high up on the Mount, where there's now the little church. The island has a vast history, Lissa. Probably enough for a television series on its own.'

His mouth curved into a teasing smile. 'Maybe you should mention that to your lord and master, Tom. And now we're speaking of him, what time do you expect the courier to arrive?'

The courier! I dropped the chocolate mint I was unwrapping and jerked upright in my chair, glancing down at my watch as I did so. If he'd left London around two o'clock, after I'd settled all the details over the phone with our Legal Department, he could be arriving any moment. Motorcycles aren't delayed by traffic in the same way as a car.

Quickly, I gathered up my bag and slipped my arms into my suede jacket. 'Aren't you going to finish your coffee?'

'No time,' I said. 'We really must get that contract signed and back to London tonight.'

'If it's so urgent, then here . . .' Daniel tossed his car key across the table to me. 'Let yourself into the Range Rover, while I settle the bill.'

'Oh, don't worry about that, Daniel. I'll pay on my credit card and charge it to expenses.'

I couldn't believe the way Daniel's expression changed. His jaw thrust out as his shoulders stiffened, and his blue-grey eyes turned to steel.

'When I asked you to have a meal with me, Lissa,' he said, his tone full of ice. 'I didn't expect it to be a business transaction. I may not have the wealth you so obviously have open access to, but I do pay my own bills.'

Feeling suitably chastened, I went outside to find the Range Rover and climbed in to wait.

Moonlight, filtering through leafless skeleton trees, patterned the frosty lanes, but I hardly noticed in my anxiety to reach the house. Daniel had travelled these roads many times and was familiar with every twist and turn, but even so the journey wasn't fast enough for me. I had to get that signed contract back to London before Tom had any chance of seeing it and querying the terms I'd arranged.

Light blazed out across the gravelled drive as we went into the house.

'Daniel?' Mrs Tregenna came slowly into the hall to meet us, wrapped in a pale blue velvet dressing gown and leaning heavily on her stick. Her usually immaculate chignon of sleek white hair hung in floating wisps around her bent shoulders. 'Oh, thank goodness you're back, my dear. I've been so terrified.'

Putting one arm round her, Daniel gently gathering her close to his side. 'What's happened, Gran? Are you all right?'

'Some young tearaway on a motorbike has been thundering on the door. I didn't open it, of course, and eventually he went away. But I found this packet on the mat. Oh, Daniel, it's not one of those terrible letter bombs you read about in the newspapers, is it? I've dialled 999 and they're sending someone over.'

My heart sank as I glanced down at the package lying on the hall table.

'Please don't be alarmed, Mrs Tregenna,' I said, stepping forward. 'It's only some documents for me. That was a courier delivering them. I'm so sorry if he frightened you. I should have warned you he was coming.'

Picking it up, I tore open the jiffy bag to reveal the stiff and heavy pages of the contract. And now the courier had gone. Even as I stood there, my mobile began to ring.

'Lissa!' Tom's furious voice barked, almost deafening me. 'What the blue blazes do you

36

think you're playing at? I've just read your text messages. Have you gone raving mad? There's no way I'm shelling out a ridiculous sum like that to tart up some impoverished Cornishman's wreck of a home. Cancel that contract immediately. And look for another location.'

Then abruptly, without giving me a moment's chance to reply, the phone clicked into silence.

CHAPTER FOUR

While I stood there, staring at the mobile phone in my hand, I suddenly realised that Daniel was looking at me, one eyebrow raised in question.

'Anything wrong?'

How could I tell him, you know all that money I told you the TV company would pay? Well, Tom has just vetoed it.

'No, nothing for you to worry about,' I lied. Only me, I thought. A siren whined, growing louder as it came up the driveway.

'That'll be the police,' Daniel groaned. 'I'd better get out there and explain it was all a mistake.'

'Well, my dear, it could have been a letter bomb. You read about these things in the newspapers all the time,' his grandmother said.

'But, Miss Thornton,' she continued, giving me a stern look, 'if you had warned me that you were expecting a parcel to be delivered by some ton-up boy riding on a motor-bike, I wouldn't have panicked and dialled 999, would I?'

'I'm so sorry, Mrs Tregenna. I really am,' I replied. 'It's all my fault. I had no idea the courier would get down here so quickly.'

If only I hadn't gone out for that meal with Daniel, I thought. If I'd been here, the contract now would be signed and on its way back to the London office. Once it was there, with any luck it would be too late for Tom to cancel when he arrived in the morning.

Now there was only one solution left to me.

The front door opened and Daniel came back into the hall, followed by a uniformed policeman.

'Sorry, Gran, but Ben insists that he has to check everything's all right. Routine procedure, he says.'

'Oh, Ben!' the old lady said, smiling winningly up at the young man, while she hastily tucked her hair back into its chignon. 'It was so silly of me. I should have looked more closely at the packet and seen it was addressed to Miss Thornton who is staying with us here. We'll forget about it, shall we, and have a nice cup of tea? I'm sure I could do with one.'

'In just a moment, Mrs Tregenna. You called me out, therefore I must follow the correct procedure, so I'd like to see this packet first, if you don't mind. Can't be too careful with things like that.'

I held out the jiffy bag containing the papers and saw him frown. 'You shouldn't have opened it, Miss. Very dangerous that could be.'

'But I knew what it contained. As Mrs Tregenna has told you, I was expecting it,' I explained. 'That's my name, there on the label, and it's addressed to here.'

Ignoring me, he turned to Daniel. 'This lady is known to you, is she, Sir?'

'Oh, Ben, for goodness's sake, stop being so officious,' Daniel said impatiently. 'Yes, of course I do. Miss Thornton is staying here. My grandmother just said that. It was a bit of a misunderstanding, that's all. Nothing to make all this fuss about.'

'Well, that's settled, isn't it, Ben?' Mrs Tregenna said, taking hold of the policeman's arm and leading him into the lounge. 'Now come along and have a cup of tea and nice slice of Mrs Tolly's saffron cake. She makes a most delicious one and I'm sure you will enjoy it.'

Giving me a doubtful look, the policeman reluctantly went with her. 'Daniel!' I called, as he went to follow them into the lounge. 'Would you read through this, then sign it, please?'

His forehead puckered slightly. 'Now?'

'Yes, now.'

Pulling a pen from his pocket, he hastily scrawled his signature at the bottom of the contract.

'You really should read it first, Daniel.

'No need. If you've done it, I'm sure it'll be okay,' he said, handing it back to me. 'Now, I'd better go and rescue Ben before my grandmother drowns him in tea. Coming?'

I shook my head. 'No, it's been a long day and I'm rather tired, so I think I'll have an early night. See you in the morning.'

Waiting until he'd closed the lounge door behind him, I tucked the document into my bag, found my car keys, and slipped out through the kitchen. Within minutes, I was travelling down the driveway, through the stone gateposts, and into the frosty moonlit lane.

* * *

At that time of night there was little traffic when I reached the A30 and could do 70mph. My main worry was finding a garage to fill up the car with petrol and the gauge was hovering close to the red danger line before I did. After that, the miles sped by but, even so, it was almost 2am before I reached London, where the streets were bright and people still jostled along the pavements.

Thankfully, I arrived at the tower block housing the company's offices where my pass-card opened the main door. But as I ran across the dark entrance hall towards the lift, an arm suddenly caught me round the chest, almost jerking me off my feet.

I'd forgotten about the security guard. Choking, I tried to pull away but his grip was too strong.

'Well now, young lady—and just what do you think you're doing?'

His second arm twisted me round and I was facing into the dazzling beam of a torch.

Fighting for breath, I gasped out, 'I . . . work . . . here.'

'Not in the middle of the night, you don't, lady.'

'Pass-card,' I gasped, trying to move my head away from the glare.

The torch beam flicked down toward my hand and I closed my aching eyes with relief.

'Melissa Thornton.' The tone of his voice changed slightly as he read the name out loud, and his grip moved to my elbow, but was just as tight.

'You do realise it's sixteen minutes after two o'clock in the morning, don't you, Miss Thornton? Rather early for you to be starting work, isn't it?'

'I know, but that's a very important document.' I nodded my head towards the packet I'd dropped as he grabbed me. 'It has to be with the Legal Department first thing. I've just driven all the way from Cornwall to get it here in time.

'And couldn't you deliver it at a normal hour, when the offices are open?'

'No, I have to be back in Cornwall by morning,' I said, straining away from the tightness of his grip. 'Look, you'd better come with me while I take it to the department. Just to make sure I'm not a terrorist about to blow up the building, or a journalist after future episodes of the soaps, or some other suspicious act.'

Still keeping hold of my arm, he bent to pick up the jiffy bag and shone the torch inside.

'All right then, Miss Thornton, there's no need to be sarcastic. As you seem to know where you're going, you can lead the way.'

I think ours was the only office building in London that decided to be environmentally friendly by switching everything off during the night—even the lift didn't work—so trying to find the right floor, let alone the right department by the light of a torch wasn't easy, not helped by having the security guard clutching my arm.

Eventually I was outside the door and, once again, my pass-card let me in to place the contract in a prominent position, with an explanatory note. I just hoped that Tom wouldn't arrive early enough to tear it up. Something I could well imagine him doing in his anger at me ignoring his orders.

After the security man had made me sign a

book, recording the time and purpose of my nocturnal visit, he escorted me out through the main door.

Then he waited on the pavement, while I started my car engine, and was driving away, before he went back inside.

Well, I thought, at least that's livened up his night a little.

*   *   *

The journey back to Cornwall seemed never-ending. I was exhausted by all the stress of the day, not just the long drive. Seeing an all-night service station, I stopped for coffee and made myself eat a ham sandwich, but several times I almost fell asleep as I drove. Luckily, the roads were almost deserted, but once an oncoming lorry blared its horn as my car veered towards it, and I managed to swerve away just in time.

Mist, like a thick grey veil, shrouded Bodmin Moor. I passed the signs to Jamaica Inn at Bolventor and could visualise Daphne de Maurier's smugglers trudging towards it in just this kind of weather.

It was still dark, but the traffic was increasing as people set off for work. Headlights suddenly appeared through the gloom and vanished quickly again. My feet and body were cold, but I dare not turn on the heater in case I really did fall asleep.

Day was edging away the darkness when I

reached Truro, the three spires of its cathedral looming above the town. By now the traffic was dense, forcing its way across roundabouts, brake-lights blazing angry red.

Almost there, I comforted myself.

I thought of Daniel, who would have been up for hours already. By now he'd be out in the fields somewhere, probably loading up the trailer. Or, with freezing hands covered in mud, cutting cauliflowers or broccoli, or daffodils and narcissi to deliver to various restaurants and markets in nearby towns.

Such a hard life, out in all weathers, helped by so very few reliable workers who were prepared to struggle on. Desperately fighting a losing battle to keep the manor house from falling into total ruin.

The fees from using it for the TV series would go a long way to help it be completed as a country house hotel, but all that now depended so much on what Tom decided to do.

I stopped at last by the edge of the sea, too tired to drive any further, and opened the car window. Tiny waves whispered along the shoreline, leaving a thin trail of seaweed. A couple of waders—greyish-brown like stones—delved long beaks into the wet sand, their dark heads bobbing rhythmically.

A thin line of gold rimmed the horizon then, as I watched, a glowing scarlet sphere began to rise and grow, until within minutes the whole sun was so bright I couldn't look at it. I closed my eyes, and slept.

Something scratching at the car door woke me and I saw the long grey muzzle of a dog resting on the open window. A voice shouted, and it was gone, racing over the sand, scattering particles upwards in fine clouds.

I glanced down at my watch—12.20—I'd slept for over four hours. Why hadn't a furious Tom rung me? He must be in the office by now and discovered what I'd done. And then I remembered. I'd switched off my mobile phone before I began to drive. Looking at it when I turned it back on, I read seven text messages. All were the same: RING ME IMMEDIATELY.

Switching it off again, I opened the glove compartment on the dashboard, dropped it inside, and closed the front. Then I climbed out of the car, locked the door, and started to walk along the beach.

Tom, and his anger, could wait.

Above me, cliffs rose, gaunt and grey, circled by gulls that seemed to hang motionless, on silent wings. The sky was a clear blue, reaching out to where the straight line of the horizon separated it from the sea. One solitary wind-surfer skimmed across the waves, like a bright red butterfly, twisting skilfully, to catch the breeze.

Taking off my shoes, I walked bare-foot along the wet sand, feeling tiny ripples shiver

45

across my toes, letting them sink into the soft coolness. Tiny shells appeared and disappeared again, as the sand moved.

I bent to pick up a wet black stone, smoothing my finger over its surface, watching it change to dull grey as it dried in the sun.

What was Daniel doing now, I wondered? Most of the spring flowers were over. Those remaining would be left in the fields to produce bulbs for the following year, and be sold during the autumn months ready to plant in people's gardens. New potatoes, his grandmother said, came next. Surely he and the Polruan family, didn't have to dig those? There must be some mechanical way of doing that. But they had to be bagged up and transported. For Daniel, it was never-ending. Season after season.

Running a country house hotel would be such a different way of life for him, and for his grandmother, too. I could imagine her, once more the lady of the manor, regal and serene. She was delightful. In just a few days I'd grown so fond of her. And her grandson.

Skimming the stone across the waves, I watched it bounce, once, twice, three times, before it sank and disappeared.

Please, I thought, turning back towards my car. Don't let that be the fate of the Tregennas and their family home.

CHAPTER FIVE

It was mid-afternoon when I returned to the house, feeling wide awake and refreshed. A builder's lorry was parked in front, with two hefty men unloading timber. One of them stopped and, pushing back his cap, came over to the car as I stepped out.

'Are you'm the television lady as phoned the gaffer yesterday?'

'Mr Pengelly? Yes, I did. Why, is there a problem?'

'Well, m'dear, we'm been stacking all this stuff in the courtyard, temporary like, only there's a good few more loads to come. So, if you'm a key, we'd best have it all indoors out of the weather. There's more rain blowing in shortly.'

'Right, I'll find Daniel and ask him,' I said, buttoning up my jacket.

Somewhere in the distance I could hear the drone of the tractor and went in that direction. I had to wait until it turned at the end of the field, where a group of three or four people were working, before I could attract Daniel's attention, and it trundled towards me.

'Lissa! Where on earth have you been?' he said, the deep lines of tiredness etched into his face easing away as he smiled. Switching off the engine, he leaned down from his seat in the cab. 'There was panic all round this morning when we couldn't find you anywhere.'

'It's a long story, Daniel. I'll tell you later but right now I need a key to the old wing. Mr Pengelly has sent up a load of materials and the men want to get it under cover, before the weather changes again.'

He whistled. 'That was quick! Pengelly usually likes to take his time. Anyway, Matty and the others can finish loading up here, while I come back with you and see what he's sent, then we can decide where to store it.'

With one easy movement, Daniel swung his long body down from the tractor cab and fell into step beside me so that I was almost running to keep up with his rapid strides.

A van had joined the lorry outside the house when we reached it, with a younger man in conversation with the other two. He walked across to meet us and held out a roughened hand.

'Mr Tregenna? I'm Paul Madron, here to check out an old staircase you want renovating.' He nodded towards the wood the men were unloading. 'Nice bit of timber Pengelly's sent up. I've just been having a look at it. Can we take it inside?'

'Hang on just a second,' Daniel said, 'while I go and fetch the key.'

After he was gone, the two workmen climbed into the lorry, reversed it, and with a belch of black exhaust fumes, it roared off down the driveway. Then it slammed to a halt, gravel spurting sideways, when a car I recognised only too well hurtled past.

Flinging open the door, Tom erupted from it, his handsome features sharp with anger.

'What the blue blazes is going on down here, Lissa? Why haven't you answered my phone calls? And what's all this about that contract going through, when I told you to abort it?'

My chin jutted. I'd done exactly what Tom ordered too many times. And that word he used—abort—was the final straw. I faced him in silence.

'Well, Lissa, I'm waiting for an answer.'

'After you've calmed down,' I replied, aware that Daniel had returned and, with Paul Madron, was watching us in amazement.

'Calmed down! Get in the car!'

'It's all right, Daniel,' I said, putting out my hand as I saw him step forward, radiating anger. 'I've no intention of going anywhere with Tom while he's in this mood. And I think Mr Madron would like to go in to see the staircase he'll be working on.'

'I want some answers. Now, Lissa!' Tom's tone was ominous and I saw his knuckles whiten as he gripped hold of my wrist.

'Why all this fuss, Tom?' I asked soothingly. 'With only ten days until you start filming, I had to act fast. You agreed the harbour is exactly what you're looking for, didn't you?

And you told me to go ahead with booking this house? Don't forget it's a genuine mine-owner's, Tom. With that sort of history, it's exactly what you need. Besides, there just isn't enough time to find anywhere else.'

I watched his shoulders relax slightly.

'That's the original wing of the house, built by one of the Tregenna mine-owners,' I continued, pointing towards one side of the building. 'You couldn't do better than that, could you? But it does need some renovation, to make it safe. You weren't answering your phone yesterday, so I had to go ahead myself and get everything started as quickly as possible. You did say I should anticipate exactly what you wanted, didn't you? That's what you pay me a ridiculous sum of money to do, isn't it?' I added, unable to resist that last dig.

Tom's gaze swung towards Daniel, who was fitting a key into the door lock. 'Well, I didn't agree to pay him a ridiculous sum of money, too.'

'But you're not only hiring Daniel Tregenna's house, Tom. I haven't seen them yet, but there are some old documents available relating to the family, as well as the house, and the mines.'

I watched a flicker of interest grow in his eyes, and went on quickly.

'You'll be gaining a wealth of genuine Cornish history that will make the series

50

completely authentic. It's not too late to make a few alterations to the script, is it? I'm quite sure that Peter will be only too pleased to have real facts to work from, making it all faction not just fiction.'

'Let's have a look at this authentic building then,' Tom said grudgingly, crunching across the gravelled drive. 'I haven't all day to waste. I've an appointment at the Maritime Museum over in Falmouth in an hour.'

'You'd better warn him about the state of the staircase, Lissa,' Daniel murmured in my ear, as he pushed open the wooden door. 'I'd really hate for him to break his neck.'

Despite all the criticism from Tom, pointing out the worst defects while we did a rapid tour of the old wing of the house, I knew him well enough to see that he was impressed. He even agreed that renovation was vital before filming began, even if it was going to be expensive, and needed to be completed as soon as possible.

'Check our insurance, Lissa. Don't want any come-back from some bit-part character breaking a fingernail,' he growled, as he climbed back into his car. 'Filming starts on the first of February. Make sure there are no hitches. A second series depends on the success of this one. And I want a second series. Remember that.'

Daniel and his grandmother seemed pleased that I was to stay on with them. And I was, too. Delighted, to be honest. Every day

51

being with Daniel, was a bonus.

Work on the oldest part of the house had to be finished quickly, but be done safely and properly. I needed to be there to make sure that it was, as well as finding other locations in the area to fit with any new storylines.

*   *   *

The following days were chaotic. Phone calls and emails winged to and fro. Several parts of the script would have to be rewritten and Peter, its writer, pacified by bringing him down to see the house for himself, to take in its atmosphere.

Mrs Tregenna was extremely helpful.

'Melissa, my dear. That documentation I mentioned to you the other day, regarding one of our ancestors who owned several mines in the area and built this house,' she said as we ate breakfast together one morning. 'His wife kept meticulous diaries. People did in those days. All hand-written, of course. Illustrated, too. Little black and white sketches. Ladies occupied many hours with that kind of activity. Nothing much else to do, I suppose. Living miles from anywhere, like this.'

'I'm sure they'd be very useful for providing background information, Mrs Tregenna. Is it possible for me to see them?' I asked.

'No problem at all, my dear. They're kept in the library.'

'In Truro or Falmouth?'

She gave a little chuckle of amusement. 'Of course not, my dear. Here, in our library. As soon as we've finished breakfast, I'll show them to you.'

I should have realised that, in a house of such size, there had to be a library and, seeing the room, I found a wealth of history stacked in leather-bound volumes on its shelves.

James Tregenna's wife, Elizabeth, had produced finely detailed pen and ink drawings of the new building to illustrate her diaries. Once it was completed and they'd taken up residence, she continued to keep a record of everyone who visited. What the ladies wore. The dinner parties they gave, with menus. Every entertainment—balls, parties, Christmas and Easter festivities, and all special occasions and events in the surrounding area.

Having scanned through several of the volumes—and they covered every year until she died, five years after her husband—I knew Peter had to see them. Here was a story in itself. All it needed was to be scripted, and there was enough material for a couple of series at least.

*　　*　　*

My only regret was that I saw so little of Daniel. He never seemed to stop working. Gone in the morning before I came down for breakfast, no matter how wet or cold the weather, while the evenings after dinner were spent in his study filling in countless forms. Every day was the same, with weekends no exception. His whole life focused on keeping the estate and house going.

But on the occasions when we did meet, the warmth of his smile wrapped itself round me and I felt a growing closeness that I'd never experienced with any man before.

While work progressed on the old wing, the refurbishment continued in the main house in preparation for its opening as a country hotel. There seemed to be workmen wherever I went. Banging and sawing echoed through every wall. Huge items were carried up and down the stairs. Mugs of tea appeared, balanced in unexpected places. Five of the remaining nine bedrooms were still being decorated and the smell of paint lingered.

Much of the original antique furniture remained, but some of the curtains and rugs covering the polished floorboards needed replacing. Luckily most rooms already had small bathrooms, but these, too, needed the modernisation that future guests would expect.

Whenever I was there, the house seemed to be full of people and noise and yet Mrs Tregenna remained placid, surrounded by all the upheaval, dust and chaos. I think she led a very solitary life and rather enjoyed the activity around her, and watching her lovely home brought back to life.

Peter, our scriptwriter for the series, arrived and took up residence in one of the newly restored bedrooms for a few days. Then, fortified by endless pots of tea, brought by a rather awestruck Mrs Tolly, he spent all his time in the library, surrounded by Elizabeth Tregenna's diaries.

'Fantastic, Lissa! Absolute gems,' was his delighted comment after a first initial reading of them. 'I can blend quite a bit of her detail into what I've already written, without too many drastic changes, and use the rest to create a second or even third series, if this one is a success.'

His freckled face grinned at me. 'Tom must be over the moon. What with the house and all this, it can't really fail, can it? Remember the Poldark series in the 70s? That kept everyone glued to their sets for weeks, and demanding more.'

*　　　*　　　*

Over the days I heard little from Tom. It was proof of his faith in me, I suppose, that he left me to get on with everything. And he was completing the filming of a short historical documentary on ferry crossings. Maritime history was one of his main interests—apart from women, of course. But maybe I'm biased about that aspect of his life.

The days didn't seem long enough. Admittedly, it was winter and got dark fairly early, but I still needed to find suitable locations for some of the future filming, so had to work closely with Peter as he re-wrote parts of the script to fit in with Elizabeth Tregenna's original detail.

Luckily, she'd recorded the names of their visitors and also their houses, as well as the villages or towns where they lived. Nearly all of them were local, and therefore fairly easy for me to track down. Persuading their present owners to let us film them was sometimes difficult, though. The fear of being burgled in the future was often uppermost in their minds.

Others couldn't be more delighted. For those whose homes now took in bed and breakfast guests, or were let out during the summer months, it would be a wonderful advertisement. And, of course, there was a fee paid if we filmed them.

The little harbour I'd found was ideal, and already some of the TV crew were transforming the surrounding buildings to create the correct historical atmosphere. Any early tourists in the area must have been puzzled at the lack of parking restriction warnings and why the telephone box was hidden behind a false wall.

Still left on my list was a visit to one of the remaining tin mines, parts of which were in the process of being turned into a tourist attraction. It was something I kept delaying.

'How about going there today?' Peter suggested as we ate breakfast with Mrs Tregenna one dark and dismal morning. 'I really need to get the feel of a place like that. It helps so much with my writing.'

'Parts of the mine go right out under the sea, you know, Lissa,' Mrs Tregenna warned. 'Quite a few disasters have occurred due to flooding in them over the years.'

'I'm sure there's no need for me to come with you, Peter,' I said quickly. Just the thought of being underground terrified me, without the additional hazard of an ocean above me as well.

'Of course there is,' he replied. 'Tom always wants to know everything about a location before he gets there, and only you can do that. You understand his needs so well, don't you, Lissa?'

He gave me a sideways look and I wondered exactly what he'd heard about the relationship Tom and I once had.

'Not today, Peter. I really haven't time,' I hedged. 'Anyway, it'll be easier for you on your own. No distractions from me asking the guide for details, to see whether it's possible for Tom to film down there, while you're trying to concentrate on the atmosphere from a miner's point of view.'

'Not scared, are you, Lissa?' he teased, wrinkling up his nose.

'Of course not!' I protested, knowing that eventually I would have to face up to my fears.

'I'm sure Daniel would take you some other time, Melissa,' Mrs Tregenna said gently, reading my expression. 'He knows those old mine workings well. His father used to take him down there quite often. It belonged to our family until quite recently, you see.'

She hesitated for a moment, before continuing. 'My son James was forced to sell it, soon after my husband died. It had been running at a loss for many years and debts had mounted up. And then, only a few months later, he and my daughter-in-law—Daniel's parents—were tragically drowned when their boat capsized in a sudden storm, off Lizard Point. Wrecked on The Manacles—a group of treacherous rocks out there.'

Her head bent for a moment, and she breathed deeply. 'As a result, now, my grandson works every hour of the day to try to keep this house, and the land around it from being sold too.'

'What wicked tales are you telling about me, Gran?' Daniel came through the door as she finished speaking, holding a mug that he filled from the silver coffee pot on the table.

'Only singing your praises, my dear,' she replied, stroking the back of his hand as she smiled fondly up at him. 'And telling Melissa that you would take her down the old mine at some time. She needs to do some research for this programme she is doing.'

'There's no rush, Daniel,' I said quickly. 'I know how busy you are.'

He looked at me thoughtfully for a moment as he sipped his coffee. 'How about tomorrow? The daffodils and narcissi are more or less over. Malty Polruan and his family can cope with the few remaining that need cutting and bunching.'

'Tomorrow,' I agreed reluctantly. 'What about you, Peter? Do you want to wait and come with us then?'

He shook his head. 'No, you're right about picking up the atmosphere on my own, without any distractions. I'll go today as we'd planned and then I can spend tomorrow at the Maritime Museum in Falmouth. I need to check out some old shipping details about how the tin and copper was transported to other regions, and the Welsh coal brought in to fire the mine engines.'

'So it'll be just you and me then, Lissa,' Daniel said quietly.

'Yes,' I murmured, trying to keep the excitement from my voice. 'Just you and me.'

CHAPTER SIX

After the greyness of the previous day, the morning was bright with sunshine when Daniel and I drove up towards the cliffs further along the coast. The tall mine chimneys rising above old engine-houses were etched against a cloudless sky and the azure sea was flecked with white-crested waves that thundered in across dark shelves of granite.

Bumping over the uneven surface of the narrow road, every now and then the Range Rover threw me sideways, and I had to resist the desire to remain leaning against Daniel's shoulder for the rest of the journey.

His strong profile was silhouetted against the car window and I could see that his eyes were fixed on the winding road ahead, the lines of tiredness half-hidden by a flop of tawny hair falling over his forehead.

I watched his long fingers, roughened by work and weather, firm on the steering-wheel, keeping the vehicle steady as it swayed round every bend.

As if aware of my intent gaze, he turned his head, and for a moment I was startled by the intensity in his eyes when he looked at me. Then, just as quickly, it was gone again, making me wonder whether I'd imagined it as he pointed out through the window towards the cliff edge.

'That's one of the old miners' tracks, Lissa. Years ago tinners led a terrible life. Tramping for miles along narrow paths, like that, in darkness and every kind of weather, to reach the mine. Then, climbing down long wooden ladders, where rungs rotted and broke away. Working, often waist-deep in water, by the light of a candle stuck to their hat. Climbing back up, at the end of a twelve-hour shift, for the long trudge back home, all for a miserable pittance of a wage. And they didn't even begin to earn a penny, until they were actually down the shaft and working.'

His jaw jerked forward as it tightened. 'Can you wonder how ashamed I feel about the way they were used by my ancestors?'

'But it wasn't you doing that, Daniel.'

'Maybe not, but I'm living in the house and on the land their hard work—and frequently their lives—provided,' he replied bitterly.

His concentration was back on the road again as the Range Rover swung sideways, down a stony track and stopped a short distance from the cliff-edge, where old mine buildings and engine-houses were clad in scaffolding, while being restored.

'Looking round you now at the bleakness of this area, you'd never think that Cornwall was once the premier tin and copper mining area in the world, would you?' he said wistfully, holding out a hand to help me climb down from the vehicle.

'Once there were well over 2,000 mines, until foreign competition took over in the 1870s. A third of the miners had no choice but to emigrate from the country, where their families had lived for generations, to find

61

work. And the Cornish industry went into rapid decline, despite a demand for tin in both World Wars.'

We were walking towards a long building now and I could feel my body begin to tense. Below me, tunnels snaked their way for miles underground. In a few minutes, I would be down there too.

An elderly, grey-haired man came out to meet us. 'Morning, young Daniel.' His gaze turned to me. 'You'm the television lady I been talking to on the phone, I dare say.'

I nodded, my mouth too dry with fear to form a reply.

'Don't usually open up to visitors this time of year, but you'm a bit special I reckon.'

He led the way into the chill of the building. 'Need a hard hat, you will. Health and Safety Regulations. You'm be all right down there on your own, Daniel? You'm probably know they mine workings better than I do.'

I felt Daniel's shoulder lean into mine as we approached an open metal cage. 'Don't look so scared, Lissa,' he whispered, his lips brushing across my ear. 'It's quite safe. We're only going to the section of the mine that's been restored. The rest would be too dangerous.'

We'd hardly stepped inside before the lift-cage dropped swiftly, rattling downwards. Panic-stricken, I closed my eyes, my fingers desperately twisting into the thick cloth of

Daniel's fleece jacket, and felt his arm slip round me, holding me firmly.

'Okay?' His voice echoed hollowly as we stepped out.

Clenching my teeth over my lower lip to prevent it quivering, I nodded.

Small lights glowed dimly in the gloom. Above and on every side was solid, glistening, damp rock. Thick wooden supports held up the low roof. Water dripped. Somewhere, not that far away I remembered, was the sea.

'Can you imagine what it must have been like down here with just the flicker of a candle?' Daniel asked, moving further down along the tunnel, away from me.

I could, but tried not to think about it. My whole mind focused on forcing one foot in front of the other to follow him. I desperately wanted to be back at the surface, breathing in cold salt air, and surrounded by open country.

The wet and slippery ground sloped and I realised, to my horror, that we were going even deeper. Our footsteps echoed in the hollow silence. I recalled superstitious tales about knockers—little creatures with arms longer than their legs—who could be heard working away, deep in a mine. Their ugly big heads were covered in grey or red hair, and they had hooked noses, squinting eyes and mouths that stretched from ear to ear. To keep them happy, miners would leave behind morsels of their food for them.

My foot tripped on a chunk of fallen rock and, looking down I saw traces of ore embedded in its rough surface. Daniel was too far ahead for me to ask him whether it was tin or copper, so I bent to pick it up and slipped it into my anorak pocket. And as I stood up again, the lights went out.

*   *   *

I couldn't believe such darkness. It was as though a thick hood had been thrown over my head. Not the slightest glimmer of light anywhere. But how could I expect there to be here, deep in the heart of the earth, surrounded only by solid rock?

Keep calm, I told myself, as I fought to control my rapid breathing. There's no reason to panic. Any second, Daniel will come back to find me.

I remembered the way the tunnels led in different directions. Like a maze. How easy it would be in the dark to take the wrong one. I must stand still.

The silence was intense, wrapping itself round me. Just the occasional drip of water. My throat tightened and I felt as though I was suffocating. Did whatever controlled the lights, control the air down here as well?

A pulse beat in my head, louder and louder. Or was it the sound of water? Was rushing water now flooding through the maze of tunnels? Pumps prevented it from doing so, but if the electricity had failed, they would stop, too, wouldn't they? And then, and then . . . My teeth bit harder into my lower lip and I tasted blood.

Oh where was Daniel? Why didn't he come back for me? And then I realised that, without light, even he wouldn't be able to find his way. He, like me, would have to stand still, rather than choose the wrong tunnel and become completely lost. So how would we ever get out? How long would it be before the guide came to find us? Did he even know the lights were out?

Miners had died down here over the years, crushed by tons of falling rock as pit props cracked and failed. Or were swept away by floods, in darkness like this. I could sense their terror. Almost hear their voices crying out. Did their ghosts haunt these narrow passages, still tapping away with their picks and shovels?

Something ice-cold touched my cheek and I screamed, hearing the sound echo round, and round, and round.

'Lissa!' Daniel's voice.

'I'm here!' I called, and my voice was a wail of anguish.

A pinpoint of light flickering, growing, filling the tunnel as it came nearer and I saw the outline of his face above the glow of a torch. My breath sighed out and my tears brimmed over, burning down my cheeks.

65

'Daniel,' I whispered, and his arms caught me as I swayed, feeling the chill of his face against mine.

'It's okay, Lissa. The lights will be back on any second now. If the electricity fails, a generator automatically takes over within five minutes.' Five minutes! Already it seemed like hours.

The sudden returning brightness was dazzling and I blinked while my eyes adjusted to it.

Daniel gently tilted my chin, brushing away the tears with one hand. 'Are you all right, Lissa? You're shaking like a leaf.'

I nodded, trying to smile. 'It's a pity Peter missed this,' I said, my voice trembling. 'He's so keen to sense the atmosphere of a place. Says it helps him make his writing true to life.' I tried to laugh, but didn't succeed very well. 'But perhaps they're intending to do this for all the tourists who visit, once the mine is reopened as an attraction.'

With Daniel's arm tight round me, holding me close to his side, I felt the laughter that rippled through him.

'Lissa, my darling, it certainly wasn't intentional. It really had me scared, so I can't imagine what it did to you.'

Lissa, my darling. That's what he said and I was sure, even in my nervous state, I didn't imagine it. *Lissa, my darling.*

His arm slid away and he gripped my hand,

his fingers warm round mine. 'Let's get you back to the surface again and find some hot coffee. You're still shivering and I don't think it's just from the cold.'

'No,' I said, stiffening my body. 'We're down here now and I do need to see for myself exactly what the conditions are like. Tom expects an answer to any question he might throw at me.'

'And what Tom says, goes. Is that it, Lissa?' I heard the bite of sarcasm in Daniel's voice.

'It's my job,' I replied quietly. 'And I aim to do it well. I'm a perfectionist—like you, Daniel.'

For a moment he was silent. 'Okay, then,' he said, reluctantly. 'If you're quite sure that's what you want and you're up to it, Lissa. Mind your head, though. This tunnel gets much narrower further along.'

Lights, like flickering candles, were tucked into niches halfway up the walls every here and there, but in between them was chill darkness. We could only walk in single-file and I struggled along, following closely behind Daniel, mentally storing up everything I saw, wishing I'd brought my pocket recorder with me.

The way in which this part of the mine was being restored, ready for opening to the public, was so authentic that I couldn't tell what was old and what was new. Thin metal rails ran along the floor where once small wagons travelled, carrying ore tipped from buckets or down a chute from where the miners were working.

I walked cautiously, head bent, gazing around me, seeing the dripping walls, smelling the dankness, hearing the distant rush of water. Daniel's footsteps echoed hollowly ahead of me and I only just saw the pale outline of his face look back occasionally. But then, suddenly, he stopped.

'What's wrong?' I said, my voice rising in panic.

'Nothing,' he replied. 'Everything's okay. I just wanted you to see this.' He was standing on a small raised platform, and leaning over a wooden rail. I moved in beside him.

'Look. Down there.'

I peered over. Below, in a hollowed out section of the rock, were three life-size models of miners. Two wore rough, open-necked shirts, rolled up at the sleeves, while the third was bare to his waist. All had trousers covered in dust, held up by thick belts, and heavy leather boots on their feet.

One of them was kneeling on the ground, tapping out a small hole in the rock wall, while another stood behind him, holding a length of quill in one hand. The third held a lighted candle.

'What are they supposed to be doing?' I asked, puzzled.

'Laying a fuse. The most dangerous job of

all.'

With his arm round my shoulders, he drew me nearer to the rail, his head so close to mine that I felt the brush of his cheek, and my breath caught in my throat.

'That goose-quill was filled with gunpowder, then lit, and they ran like the devil to get away before the explosion blew out the rock face. Frequently, the quill burnt too quickly and exploded. Many a miner was lacking fingers, or lost a hand or even his life. But there was always some other poor wretch waiting to take on the job, rather than let his family starve, as many did in those days.' His jaw went taut against my cheek and I sensed the pain, and anger, he was feeling. 'All to fill the pocket of some rich mine-owner, who never even got his hands dirty.'

'You mustn't feel such guilt, Daniel.'

His voice and eyes were full of torment, when he looked back at me. 'But I do, Lissa. My family, my ancestors, living off the hardship of men, women and even children, who knew no other way to survive.'

'Is that why you're out there, all hours of the day, in all weathers, labouring beside those people who work for you in the fields?'

'I don't expect them to do anything I wouldn't do myself, Lissa. And even then, they earn their money in a way few would want to do nowadays, just because in past years their families have always worked on the estate.

69

And what saddens me most is that they feel privileged to do so.'

'Oh, Daniel!' I said, raising my hand to smooth his taut cheek.

His fingers caught mine, gripping them tightly, his arm pulling me closer, his head turning slowly towards mine, and I closed my eyes, waiting . . . 'Daniel!'

Through the tunnel came the echo of footsteps. Abruptly, Daniel stepped back, and I heard his breath sigh out as the guide appeared.

'You'm all right, Daniel? Sorry about that breakdown with the lighting. Now, I'll have to hurry you along. Some of the men need to get working down here. There be more of they figures to set up and it do take a fair bit of time getting it all just right.'

'Sorry, Jack. I should have realised. Will it be okay if Lissa comes back some other time? She'll need to bring her boss down to show him what it's like, and whether it's possible for filming.'

'A film? Of us'm working, you mean?' Jack's wizened face brightened as he smiled, revealing a set of crooked teeth.

'No, Jack, it would be actors, I'm afraid,' Daniel replied regretfully.

'But some of your men might be used as extras, Jack,' I added.

'Might I be one of they?'

'Well, it all depends on whether Tom

70

decides he can film down here,' I said. 'Let's keep our fingers crossed, shall we?'

'Me, a film star! That would be summat special to tell my grandchildren, now, wouldn't it?'

'Now, Lissa,' Daniel said. 'Let's get you back up to the surface and find some coffee.'

* * *

The sun was high over the sea, turning it into a sparkling shimmer of colour when Daniel stopped the Range Rover outside a little café in the nearby village.

'Have you eaten a Cornish pasty yet?' Daniel asked me enthusiastically.

I shook my head, my mind still lost in the echoing darkness of the mine as we entered the low-beamed room, where a log fire crackled and blazed at the far end, and old farming implements hung on the rough white walls.

'Then you should, and this is the place to eat one. Jenna Merryn bakes the tastiest in Cornwall, don't you?' he said, smiling at the elderly lady who came to greet us, dusting flour from her hands.

'If you say so, young Daniel, but don't you let my daughter-in-law hear you. She reckons hers are the best over in Penzance. What can I get you?'

He raised a questioning eyebrow in my

direction.

'How can I resist after such a recommendation?' I said.

'Then it's two pasties and coffee, please, Jenna.'

I watched her disappear through a curtained doorway and settled myself more comfortably on the long cushioned bench. The room was part of an old terraced cottage, homely with chintz and wooden wheel-back chairs.

'I'm sorry you had such a scare down there,' Daniel said, the bench creaking as he sat down beside me. 'You must have been petrified. I was, and I know that mine and all its passages pretty well.'

'Well, now I understand what it was like for the miners of olden days.'

'Do you?' he said doubtfully. 'Boys as young as eight worked down there, ten hours a day, six days a week. And with consumption, bronchitis or rheumatism, let alone injury, a miner rarely survived beyond forty.'

'But it did provide work for whole families in the area, didn't it?' I reasoned. 'From the research I've been doing, once mining ceased, there's been nothing left to replace it. Even the fishing industry has declined because of all the new rules and regulations. All you've got left in Cornwall now is tourism.'

'And my pasties,' chuckled Jenna, coming back with a loaded tray.

72

'They smell good, Jenna,' Daniel said, taking the plates from her and putting one in front of me. 'You like your coffee strong, don't you, Lissa?'

As the warmth of the room surrounded me, I began to feel better, and the pasty really was delicious.

'Do you know why they have this thick crusty edge?' Daniel asked.

With my mouth full of the savoury mixture, I could only shake my head.

'Arsenic was also found in the mines and a miner's hands would be coated with it as he worked. Because they'd no time to come to the surface, he took his main meal of the day with him—a pasty with meat at one end and apple filling at the other—his wife made it with a thick edging for him to hold, which he then threw away after eating the rest.' Daniel thoughtfully studied the piece left in his hand. 'And 'tis said that rats living in the mine gobbled up the crumbs and were poisoned by the arsenic.'

'Don't forget to tell all this to Peter,' I said, brushing a flake of pastry from my lap. 'Any snippets like that are gold dust to him.'

'Are you ready to go home now?' The wooden bench creaked again as Daniel stood up.

'I suppose so,' I said reluctantly.

Being with him in this lovely secluded room, I felt completely relaxed, content to stay there for ever, enjoying his company. He was such a gentle man, thoughtful and kind, too. Not the type of man I usually met in my everyday life. Maybe living here in Cornwall, away from the rest of the world, had that effect.

He laughed, his grey-blue eyes crinkling at the corners. 'You don't sound too sure. Why? Is there somewhere else you want to see? I'm making this a rare day off, Lissa, so we'd better make the most of it.'

I hesitated. Daniel was a busy man. And yet . . . I wanted to be with him for a while longer. Soon, Tom would be here to start filming. Then I'd be back at his beck and call and have no time for anything else.

'Would the tide be right to cross the causeway to St Michael's Mount?'

'It should be,' Daniel said, his mouth widening into a smile that made my heart beat faster. He held out his hand. 'Come on. Let's go and see.'

CHAPTER SEVEN

It didn't take long to reach Marazion and by the time the Range Rover was bumping over cobbles into the car park by the sea wall, the castle was sharply silhouetted against the sky.

'Just like a fairytale,' I breathed, gazing across the narrow stretch of sea to where it rose, high on its island, remembering how I'd seen it the evening Daniel and I had dinner together at the hotel by the water's edge. 'It looks even more romantic by daylight.'

'I always forget just how magical it can seem to people who've never seen it before,' Daniel said, following my gaze. 'It is quite spectacular though, isn't it?'

The tide had receded on either side of a stone path that wound across from a cluster of rocks by the sandy beach, to where a row of terraced houses lined one side of a tiny harbour. Already tourists were walking along it, avoiding tiny pools and strands of still-wet, slippery seaweed.

We were only just crossing the sand towards the causeway when my mobile phone began to ring. I guessed who it would be, even before I heard his voice.

'Lissa! Where the blue blazes are you?'

'Hi, Tom,' I said, but before I could continue, he was already rushing on. 'I'm at the house. Wherever you are, get back here. Now!'

I was surprised to read the cold expression in Daniel's eyes, when I explained, and we turned round to return to the Range Rover.

'Of course,' he said, and his voice was toneless. 'When Tom says jump, you jump, don't you, Lissa?'

'I do work for him,' I replied defensively.

'So what's the attraction? There must be

something for you to act like this all the time,' he said, unlocking the door of the car.

'Attraction?' I questioned, my back stiffening defensively as I climbed in to the Range Rover and did up the seatbelt, studiously not looking at Daniel.

'Something must keep you working for a man who treats you so abominably. Are you in love with him?'

For a moment I was silent. Daniel's head turned, and the look he gave me was challenging. 'Are you?'

'I thought I was. Once, a long time ago. Soon after I'd started working for him. I didn't know then that Tom was a womaniser. Or that he regarded any new girl as a trophy for him.'

I paused, not wanting to continue.

The engine roared into life as Daniel pressed his foot hard down on the accelerator, and the car moved over the bumpy ground towards the road. 'You had an affair?'

'Not an affair,' I said quickly. 'It wasn't like that. Tom was directing a documentary on French composers. I'd just joined the TV company, still in training. One night, when we were in Paris, he took me out to dinner as a thank you, he said, for the excellent work I'd done. At seventeen, I was easily flattered and Tom is a very attractive man. It was a lovely meal, but I wasn't used to drinking so much wine.'

I saw Daniel's profile sharpen. 'And you

slept together,' he said abruptly.

'Yes, we did. I don't remember much about it. But I made quite sure it never happened again. Now we work together. Nothing more.'

The Range Rover gathered speed as we left Marazion and reached the main road. Daniel drove in silence, but I knew I couldn't leave it there. I had to tell him the rest of the story.

'It wasn't long after that when I realised I was pregnant.'

The car jerked and I saw his fingers whiten as they tightened round the steering-wheel. 'You have a child?'

'No. Tom insisted on an abortion. I was just starting out, with a fantastic career ahead of me, so I did what he instructed.'

'Do you regret it?' The anger dissipated from Daniel's voice suddenly, leaving it gentle.

'Every day of my life. A few months later I had a complete breakdown and was admitted for psychiatric care and counselling.'

'Yet you went back to work for him?'

'Not at first,' I said. 'I moved around the company for a few years, gaining more experience, then Tom needed a new researcher and my name was put forward. It was a brilliant promotion. No one knew what had happened. How could I turn it down?' I looked defiantly across at Daniel's taut expression. 'And I'm good at my job.' My voice lowered. 'Besides, I'd had to grow up a lot in those intervening years, too—developed a thicker skin. I had to.'

We'd turned off the main road into the lane leading back to the house before Daniel spoke again.

'Lissa, how old would your child have been now?'

His words jolted through me. I didn't want to answer. I could guess what he was thinking. Very slowly, I replied. 'Almost four years old.'

But it didn't add up with the age of the child I see in my room every night. We continued the journey in silence.

When Tom came out onto the driveway to meet us, his tone was cutting. 'I don't pay you a small fortune to joy-ride round the countryside with your new boyfriend, Lissa.'

Not daring to look at Daniel, I felt colour flame into my cheeks, and my chin jutted. 'Daniel and I have been up to the tin mine to see whether it's suitable to film,' I said, my voice sharp with anger.

'And you couldn't drive there yourself?' he asked sarcastically.

Daniel moved forward to face him, his whole body tight with restrained fury. 'The mine once belonged to my family. I know every inch of it, which is why I went with Lissa. And I don't think you should film down there. It would be far too risky. The conditions just aren't suitable. You'd do better with a mock-up, or whatever you call.

Tom's lips thinned. 'You're an expert, are

you?'

'I certainly know far more about mines that you do.'

'But not about filming, Mr Tregenna.' Tom pointedly turned his back on Daniel and caught hold of my wrist. 'I want you and Peter, with the new scripts and locations, in the library in five minutes. Too much time's been wasted with you lazing around. Well, don't just stand there thinking about it, Lissa. Go and fetch Peter. Now!'

I couldn't meet Daniel's eyes, remembering his earlier words. 'When Tom says jump, you jump, Lissa.' He's so right, I thought. What must he think of me? But then, I reasoned, why should he even think of me at all? Especially now, after everything I've told him.

*   *   *

Peter couldn't wait to show Tom the Tregenna diaries.

'So much minute detail in them, Tom. They're amazing.' Carefully he turned to one of the pages. 'Just look at this drawing. Those women, every item of their dresses, their shoes, their hair styles, even the way the room is arranged. It's all there for you, Tom. Absolutely authentic, recorded at the time. The Wardrobe department is going to love these.'

'Buy them off the old lady then, but keep

79

the price low. We're paying through the nose in any case for using this place—thanks to Lissa here.'

'You can't do that, Tom,' I protested angrily. 'These diaries are part of this family's history. There's no way Mrs Tregenna will sell them.'

'People can be persuaded to do anything, provided you pay them, Lissa. You should know that only too well.'

His meaning was quite plain, and heat flared into my face. 'Now, run along and have a word with her. Then get these drawings scanned and email them up to London.'

'No way,' I retorted. 'The pages are much too fragile to take that. You agree don't you, Peter?'

Gently closing the volume, he nodded.

'Well, we're not going to need them afterwards, so what does it matter?' Tom growled.

'It matters to the Tregennas,' I said angrily. 'Surely, Peter, they can be photographed and then email the photographic copies, can't you?' I asked.

'No problem.'

'Anyway, Tom,' I said, heading for the door. 'As Daniel says it's not going to be possible to film down the mine. I'll get on to Scenery to make a start on creating something right away.'

'Hang on a minute, Lissa. I decide what's

going to be possible or not.'

I stared back at him. 'But Daniel said it was too risky. You heard him.'

Tom's lip curled. 'Ha! So I'm supposed to take the word of a country yokel like that, am I? Just because he was once lord and master of all he surveyed? Who the blue blazes does he think he is, telling me what to do? Get moving, Lissa. We're going up there right now.'

'It's getting late, Tom. Leave it until tomorrow,' I suggested.

'I said, now, Lissa.'

*　　*　　*

Some of the men were already leaving when Tom's car roared up in front of the mine buildings, and I saw Jack come out to meet us.

'Hi, Jack,' I said, unclipping my seat belt and climbing out. 'Daniel told you that I'd need to bring my boss here, didn't he? Well, here we are.'

'I'm sorry, miss, but we'm just closing up for the day. 'Tis getting dark.'

'Well, that's not going to make any difference down a mine, is it?' Tom snapped. 'Come on, man. I haven't got all day to waste.' He pulled a wallet from his inside pocket and took out a handful of notes. 'Here. That should cover any overtime for you.'

I watched Jack's mouth tighten. 'Don't need no bribery, sir. If this young maid says you'm

81

should go down for a viewing, then down you'm shall go, and I'll take you myself.'

Back inside the building, Jack switched on the lights and handed us hard hats to put on. Tightening the strap under his chin, Tom strode across to the lift cage, his eyes eager with anticipation.

Reluctantly, I followed, my legs already shaking at the thought of going into those underground tunnels again.

'This is fantastic!' Tom shouted as the lift dropped rapidly, and I clung to its metal bars in panic.

As we stepped out into the maze of tunnels, Tom growled impatiently, 'Which way? Come on, man. Get moving. I've a series to produce.'

'Don't you be rushing, sir. 'Tisn't safe to be rushing head-long down passages like these be. Roof gets low ahead of you. Stand back and let me be leading the way.'

It was the same route that Daniel had taken me earlier that day and when we reached the spot where the lighting had failed, my heart began to pound, but this time all was well. I could see Tom's head flicking impatiently from side to side, as he viewed everything we passed. Now and then he stopped to peer down other darkened passages.

'What about this one?' he barked, moving towards a low tunnel. 'Where does that lead?'

Jack spun round. 'No, sir. Just you'm stay on the marked route. Those be old workings. Not open to the public.'

'But I'm not the public, am I, man? If my programme is to be authentic, then I shall need to film where these events would have taken place, not some tacky trail laid on for tourists. Now, you've a torch, haven't you?'

Reluctantly, delving into a pocket, Jack produced one.

'Right then. Lead on.'

'I be warning you, sir. 'Tisn't safe. They pit props been there centuries. Can't be sure how long they'll hold up.'

'Rubbish!'

Snatching the torch from Jack, Tom shone it round the dripping walls.

'Now, this really is something. None of your plastic models and artificial candles. It'll be real people and real candles for my filming. Right. This is the area we'll be using.'

I blinked as the beam of the torch swung across my vision.

'Lissa! What the blue blazes are you doing, shivering away back there? Sort out the arrangements with whoever runs this place in the morning.'

'But sir . . .' Jack began.

'Start moving, man, back to the surface. I don't have time to be hang about. I've a lot to do.'

When I told Daniel about the visit, later in the evening, he was furious.

'The man's mad! That area of the old

workings has had nothing done to it for years. It has to be regarded as unsafe. He'll never get permission.'

But Daniel didn't know Tom, or his methods of persuasion. 'Money buys anything, and anyone' was his motto, and I knew from past experience that he always won. I comforted myself that only a very few of the scenes would actually be shot in the mine. No one would be down there long enough for any disaster to happen.

*   *   *

From then on, Tom took over. He was the director, that was his job.

I'd done my part now and what I had left to do now was make sure each location was available and ready at the point in filming when he needed it.

And now, once again, the child was in my room each night, seeming to move closer with every appearance, so that I could see the shape of its little face and the heartbreaking sadness in its wide eyes, haunting my sleep.

Leading members of the cast were beginning to arrive, already well-rehearsed in their parts. With most of the rooms in the house finally restored, ready for its opening at Easter, they and Tom took up residence.

Minor actors were lodged all around the neighbouring area, to the great delight of the local B&Bs for whom this was usually their slack season.

Mrs Tolly, and those training to be hotel staff, coped uncomplainingly with everything—and some of those actors could be very demanding. But after a few days in their company, Daniel's grandmother, Mrs Tregenna, declared the lounge to be for her use only and quietly retired into her own part of the house.

Of Daniel, I saw little.

He should be pleased, I told myself crossly. I've brought him all these guests, even before the house is officially open as an hotel. But I knew such an invasion wasn't what he'd planned when creating it. Ordinary guests wouldn't be like this.

Telling Daniel had dredged up long-hidden memories of my lost baby and I'd hoped, in doing so, it might prevent my nightmares—if they were nightmares. But now they were worse. I began to dread going to bed, knowing that just as I was drifting into sleep, the child would be there. And it was my child—it had to be, created by my guilt. There was simply no other logical explanation.

*   *   *

Filming began in February. The days grew longer. The weather brighter. Spring in Cornwall is always early. Primroses covered the high banks of the lanes and hid under hedges that were misted with green. As the weeks passed bluebells massed the woods and foxgloves grew tall. Honeysuckle twined through the hedgerows, and the cliff tops were pink with thrift and yellow vetch.

Even Tom had to admit, grudgingly, that the location was perfect.

Easter was in March that year, and with it came the official opening of the hotel. One of the most popular of the leading actors cut a ribbon across the front door. Mrs Tregenna, wearing an amazing hat lent to her by the wardrobe department, stood regally beside him, for all the photographs.

I hardly recognised Daniel, as he stood behind her for the ceremony. His tawny hair had been neatly trimmed, though still remained long. Immaculate in a dark suit, with crisp white shirt and blue patterned tie.

He looked completely different from the tall, rangy and slightly unkempt figure in faded sweatshirt and jeans that I'd now grown to know so well. And had grown so distant, too.

Reports and photographs appeared in all the local newspapers, and eventually reached some of the Sunday supplements. The Cornish tourist season was underway.

Once people read in the press about the connection with the forthcoming TV series, starring such well-known names, they booked rooms for weeks in advance. Our film sets were thronging with curious onlookers, eager to know what was happening and perhaps catch a glimpse of one of the actors.

Good publicity, Tom gloated. The series would go out on TV in June, every Sunday, for six weeks. And, if successful, Peter had more than enough material to script further episodes.

Daniel became more remote from me, as if making quite sure our paths never crossed. With the hotel to run and supervise, I knew he was busy preparing Matty Polruan to deal with the planting or harvesting crops out in the fields, but it saddened me that our growing closeness had come to an end so abruptly. Was it because of what I'd told him, or that Tom was there, ruling my life again?

*　　*　　*

It had been a particularly exhausting day. One of the principal actors, who played the mine-owner, slipped when coming down the newly-restored staircase in the old wing of the house. Tom insisted I drove the man to Truro Hospital to be checked over.

'Can't afford him putting in some inflated insurance claim,' he growled. 'But make sure his name, and that the accident occurred during filming of the series, get a mention in the Press.'

Having spent most of the afternoon waiting

for X-rays and to see a doctor, we were caught up in a long queue of traffic, after a caravan overturned in one of the narrow lanes. When we finally arrived back at the house, Tom was pacing up and down, his expression furious.

'At last!' he roared, 'Why the blue blazes didn't you phone me, Lissa? I've been cooling my heels here, with no clue whether we can continue filming that scene, or need to move on to another location.'

'He's fine,' I soothed. 'Just a slight sprain, that's all. They've strapped it up and said if he rests it for the remainder of the day, it'll be okay to walk on by tomorrow, so there should be no problem. I know it's getting late, but why not film the evening sequence where young Josh arrives on horseback in the courtyard? The sun should be in the right position in an hour or so.'

'If you'd contacted me earlier, we could've had it all set up by now.'

'Well, there's still plenty of time,' I answered.

'Don't hang about, then. You'll need to call that woman with the horses.'

As she ran a riding school, and it was the school holidays, all the horses were out, so it took another couple of hours before a suitable one appeared, only just in time to be filmed before the sun began to set.

That didn't improve Tom's temper.

*   *   *

The dining room, where previously I'd always eaten with Mrs Tregenna and Daniel, was now part of the hotel, so they ate together at a small table in her lounge.

Mrs Tolly, as well as looking after the old lady, assisted the newly-appointed chef in the kitchen.

Behaving like he was lord of the manor, Tom had taken over the original long table in the centre of the room, joined by the principal actors.

Filming the series was coming to an end. Several of them would soon be leaving to rehearse for the summer season of plays at Chichester Theatre. Remaining scenes would be shot back in the studio.

'Lissa!' Tom's voice rang out over the hubbub of chatter filling the dining room, as I went to join Peter and a few of the production team. 'Here!'

He beckoned to one of the waiters. 'Another chair!' Reluctantly, I moved towards him and I found myself sitting next to him.

'What would I do without her?' he said, waving his wine-glass in the air and putting his arm round my shoulders. 'Keeps me on the straight and narrow, don't you, Lissa?'

He aimed a wet kiss at my cheek and I ducked my head, avoiding it. 'Well, it's Durham next, my love. Once we've finished here in a day or so, you need to be up there checking out the cathedral, ready for my series on ancient architecture.'

A day or so? I was stunned. Tom had given me no prior warning. In a couple of days I'd be leaving Cornwall, moving on. But that was my job. New locations, new research, constantly changing. That's what I loved about the work, wasn't it? Well, wasn't it?

I glanced round the huge room, even more beautiful since its renovation. How was I going to leave it all behind? And Daniel.

The menu, as always, was excellent, but my throat felt too tight to eat and I pushed away the delicately arranged starter of cream cheese wrapped in smoked salmon on its bed of salad leaves, without even tasting it. I refused the chicken chasseur, and only tried a spoonful of the lemon roulade. Even the coffee seemed bitter.

Strident voices and raucous laughter filled the whole room, pulsing through my head. Tom's being the loudest of all.

By nine o'clock my head was aching and I decided to have a long relaxing bath. Maybe then I'd sleep deeply enough to avoid any nightmares.

Tom's fingers suddenly gripped my wrist tightly as I stood up. 'Not leaving us so soon, are you, Lissa? An early night, is that it?'

Pulling my arm away, I nodded.

*　　　*　　　*

The house was silent when I woke, with moonlight making a silver path across the floor of my room. Yet I knew something had woken me. Not the child this time. The room was empty. And then I heard a movement and, turning over, saw Tom sitting in the chair beside my bed. For once, I'd been so tired I'd forgotten to lock my door.

'This is just like old times, eh, Lissa?' he slurred, now obviously drunk.

'Please go, Tom,' I managed to say.

He rose to his feet, swaying slightly, and leaned across the bed, his hand dragging back the covers.

'A celebration, Lissa. Reward for good work. Like we did once before all those years ago.' He threw back his head and laughed. 'Surely you don't think I've forgotten?'

'Tom!' I said, trying not to breathe in the fumes of alcohol. 'Please go.'

'Not yet, my love. Or are you expecting that Cornish yokel to join you? Is that it? A nightly romp in this delightful four-poster? Well, remember, I was here first, Lissa. Don't you ever forget that.'

His fingers slid over my body, clutching at the folds of my cotton nightdress, his sour breath filling my nostrils.

'Tom!' I shrieked, twisting myself sideways, away from him.

My outstretched arm hit the bedside table, my hand catching the rough surface of the lump of ore I'd found in the mine, and kept as a reminder of that special day with Daniel. Gripping it, I swung it across, hearing the dull thud as it met Tom's head.

With a bellow of anger, he stepped backwards, knocking over the chair and it fell to the floor with an echoing crash.

'You little vixen!' he roared.

'Now, get out!'

Stumbling, as he crossed the room, he opened the door and it slammed behind him, leaving me shaking.

That's the end, I decided. No job is worth such humiliation.

CHAPTER EIGHT

Tom brushed aside any questions about the gash across his forehead the next morning, saying he'd walked into a door, and I didn't reveal the truth. Maybe I should have done. But it would be his word against mine, and his status was far superior.

'I need to speak to you, Tom,' I said, going up to his table as he was eating breakfast.

'Fire away then,' he replied, cutting into a slice of bacon.

I glanced round at the others sitting with

him. 'Alone. When you've finished. I'll be in the library.'

'So, why all the secrecy?' he asked, entering the room. 'Oh, come on, Lissa! It's not about last night, is it? Forget it. I was drunk.' He put his hand to his head. 'But I could take you to court for assault, you know.'

'I'm leaving, Tom.'

'I know all that. You're going up to Durham, but not for another couple of days yet. There's stuff for you to finish off here first.'

'I'm leaving the company. Now. Today,' I repeated. 'I've been under your thumb for far too long, Tom. You're just an arrogant bully who thinks he can buy his way into whatever he wants. Well, I'm not going to be a part of that any more.'

'But this job, Lissa, it's you to a T. You're fantastic. Half the time, you carry me. I can't work without you. Look, if it's an increase in salary you want, that's fine. Just name your price and it's yours.'

I laughed. 'Oh, yes, Tom, it all comes down to money with you, doesn't it? Anyone will do anything for money, isn't that what you're always saying. Well, not me. Not any more. Once you bought the life of my unborn child. I'll never forgive you for that.'

'So it's the Cornish yokel now, is it?' he sneered. 'I should've guessed.'

'No, Tom. I only wish it was,' I replied sadly.

93

'Daniel has no interest in me whatsoever. Why would he? Our lives are so very different. Mine, an entirely artificial world. And his . . .'

'That of a mud-caked country bumpkin, content to be rattling round on a broken-down tractor, grubbing up vegetables for a living.'

'Not with the hotel up and running,' I protested hotly. 'The Tregennas' lives are going to change for the better now.'

'Thanks to my generosity,' Tom put in. 'Without all the money I paid out to have this place put to rights again, it would have been a tumble-down ruin within months. And where would your lord of the manor been then, I'd like to know? Out on his neck—and the old lady with him.'

'Well, don't forget that the money you—or rather the company—paid out was for your TV series. Without this house and all its history, you'd never have created anything as brilliant as it's going to be. And it will be a success, Tom. I'll grant you credit for that. You're a great director.'

He caught hold of my arm. 'Then stay on, Lissa,' he pleaded. 'We're a good team. Without you, I'd never have found this place in a thousand years. I need you.'

'I'm sorry, Tom, but I've made up my mind. Nothing you say is going to change that. Now I have to pack.'

His expression was rigid as he strode towards the door but, before opening it, he spun round. 'You'll finish what you're paid to do first. Make sure this area is back to its original state before you leave, or there'll be serious trouble.'

He was right. That was something still I had to do—it was part of my job and my responsibility.

*   *   *

Later, when I came back from the harbour, where I'd been arranging for a crew to remove all our changes there, Daniel was cutting the lawns, his tawny hair damp on his forehead as he strode behind the motor mower. I climbed out of my car and sat on one of the wooden benches to watch him.

In another day, I'd never see him again. The pain of it tore through me.

He reached the end of the lawn and switched off the mower, hesitating for a moment, before walking slowly across to where I was sitting.

I watched every movement of his long body; the way he brushed a hand across his cheek to remove bits of clinging grass; the smile that was tilting his mouth. Storing every detail in my memory.

'I don't know if you've heard but May eighth is Flora Day in Helston, Lissa,' he said, and I felt the warmth of his arm brush against mine as he sat down beside me. 'It's a magical day.

Will Tom be filming it for the series?'

I shook my head, trying to hold back the tears that brimmed threateningly in my eyes. 'The company will be gone by then.'

His forehead puckered in a puzzled frown. 'Gone?' he said hollowly.

'Hasn't Tom told you yet? Filming is virtually finished. Just a couple of retakes down the mine. They came out too dark.'

He didn't seem to be listening. 'You're leaving?'

'Yes. Today. I've quit my job.' I tried to smile. 'So you see, when Tom says jump, I won't be jumping any more.'

Daniel's eyes were like grey clouds as he studied me thoughtfully for a moment. 'We never did the cross to St Michael's Mount, did we, Lissa?'

I swallowed the lump tightening my throat. 'No, Daniel, we never did.'

'Then let's go now.'

'Now? But . . .'

'No buts, Lissa. Come on.'

He stretched out a hand and pulled me to my feet.

*   *   *

The causeway was still partly covered when we parked by the sea wall. A few small boats were taking people to and fro, depositing them over at the harbour or by the rock steps at

Marazion.

'Take off your sandals. It won't be deep.'

Obediently, I did as Daniel said, rolled up the bottom of my jeans and, holding his hand, waded into the shallow water. Tiny waves slid across the stone path, warm round my ankles, and I looked up into his laughing eyes, wishing that once we reached the island, we could stay there for ever, cut off from the rest of the world.

'Wait a second. Have you brought any money with you?' he asked suddenly. 'We have to pay to go up to the castle and I didn't need any for mowing the lawn.'

As I reached into the pocket of my denim jacket, my foot slipped sideways on a strand of seaweed, throwing me off-balance. Daniel swung round, his arm catching me before I sank into the water and we stood, swaying for a moment, clinging tightly to each other, my forehead resting against the warmth of his skin.

Time hung suspended, even the sound of the sea was muted. Daniel's fingers gently tilted my chin, his face bending down to mine, so, so slowly. I watched a whisper of breeze tangle a lock of hair across his forehead, saw the pupils of his eyes widen and grow black before they closed, felt the slight stubble that shadowed his upper lip, before our mouths met, then parted, then met again.

The touch of his lips was gentle, feathering

over mine, deepening into a kiss I didn't want to ever end.

'Ooh look, Mavis, this is better than going to the pictures,' a voice said, and we pulled apart reluctantly to see two elderly ladies, their dresses held high above their white dimpled knees, paddling across the sand behind us. 'Don't take no notice of us, dears. It's nice to see a bit of a cuddle. Envious that's all we are.'

Chuckling, they continued on their way and, hand in hand, we followed them, avoiding rocks as we reached the island. Then came the steep, rough climb to the top, stopping breathlessly every now and then to look back at the growing trail of people crossing the causeway, with the sea rapidly receding on either side.

Daniel was silent. His hand still holding mine. Was he regretting that kiss, I wondered? It had seemed such a natural thing to do. Maybe now, though, he was remembering what I'd told him about Tom and me—and the baby.

The view from the top of the island was amazing. Endless sea crinkling away to the dark line of the horizon in one direction. Marazion, with its softly coloured houses bordering the pale sand, in the other.

We toured the main rooms of the castle. Then spent a while in the little chapel, where the sun, shining through the stained glass windows, created jewel colours of red, blue, green and gold to pattern Daniel's tawny hair.

As we stood there, together, I could almost hear the whisper of centuries of prayer held in the thick granite of its walls. Outside again, standing on the battlements, we were watching black and white oyster-catchers down on the rocks below, when my mobile phone rang.

Oh, surely not! Why did Tom have to spoil such a perfect afternoon? With a quick glance up at Daniel's frown, I pressed the key.

But it wasn't Tom's barking voice. It was one of his film crew who gabbled a few words.

I turned to Daniel, my heart pounding. 'There's been an accident at the mine,' I told him. 'We need to get over there quickly.'

It's surprising neither of us twisted an ankle or slipped as we scrambled back down the path, ran across the causeway, to where the Range Rover was parked, and drove, far too fast, up to the mine.

Two police cars, an ambulance and fire-engine blocked the main entrance when Daniel stopped close behind them. A policeman ran across, waving his hands.

'Can't park there, Mr Tregenna, sir. Official vehicles only.'

Ignoring him, Daniel jumped out. 'What's happened, Jack?' he asked, as the elderly guide I'd met on my previous visits came hurrying out.

'That stupid dunderhead that's been making a film down there. You'd warned him and I'd warned him not to use that old section of the mine. It isn't safe. But he goes ahead. Thinks he knows best.'

'So what's happened?' Daniel repeated impatiently.

'Decided to shift one of they pit props out of his way and brought down part of the roof.'

'Anyone hurt?' Daniel asked, striding swiftly towards the mine entrance.

'Passage is blocked, with two of them still behind it. Wait, Daniel! You can't go down there! It's too dangerous.'

But it was far too late. He had already gone.

'Daniel!' I cried, trying to follow, but the policeman caught my arm, preventing me from following.

'Leave him, Miss. He probably knows this mine better than any of us, and the workings of it.'

Another ambulance raced across the rough ground, its siren wailing, and two paramedics ran into the building.

'Let me go in,' I pleaded, turning towards the policeman. 'I'm part of the TV team. I need to keep up to date with what's going on.'

He eyed me doubtfully, then relented. 'Okay then, Miss. Just inside though, but no further. And stay out of everybody's way. My governor will have my guts for garters if you don't.'

The young actor who was playing the leading tin miner, four extras used as some of the others, and a member of the camera crew, were huddled in blankets at one end of the room, their faces pale and streaked with dirt.

'How did it happen?' I asked, running across to them.

The camera man coughed and cleared his throat. 'You know Tom, Lissa,' he said. 'Everything has to be spot-on. He decided the stuff we filmed a couple of weeks ago was too dark. Remember—that bit where they're setting explosives to open up a new seam? So down we go to do a re-take. Mr Tregenna and old Jack warned us, right from the beginning, not to use that old part of the mine.'

He wiped a grimy hand across his chin and I saw blood caked over his knuckles. 'Tom wanted a shot in the narrowest part of the tunnel. Phil's camera got jammed between a pit prop and the wall, wouldn't budge.' The man shook his head in disbelief. 'So what does Tom do? Only gets everyone to try to shift the prop. "Get it out of the way," he said.'

'And?' I prompted.

'What d'you think, Lissa? Bloody roof comes down. That's what. Him and Phil under it.'

'But the rest of you got out safely?'

'Only because we were on the other side. If Phil was still filming, Tom'd have his authentic shots right enough.'

'Not much good if he's dead though, is it?' one of the extras muttered. A bleak silence filled the room. No one looked at each other.

I remembered the terrible claustrophobic feeling when the lights went out. What must it be like with dust-filled air in such a tiny cramped space, and the threat of more falling rock?

Oh, why did Daniel go down there, too? Why risk his life for people that meant nothing to him? How could I bear it, if anything happened to him?

It was only months since I'd arrived in Cornwall. Only months since I first met Daniel. And yet it seemed as though I'd always known him. That he'd always been a part of my life.

Why did I care so much about what happened to him? In another day I'd be back in London, starting another chapter of my life, trying to find another job. Maybe even going abroad. With so many changes in the media, the TV world was shrinking.

I'd forget Daniel. Forget Daniel? But I'd never forget him. How could I when I loved him so much?

I closed my eyes, trying not to think of what was happening far below the ground. Even now Daniel could be desperately trying to force a way through the rocks blocking the tunnel. With the prop gone, the roof could collapse further, crashing down, crushing him.

Was it dark down there? Had the lighting failed with the rock fall? Was water already creeping in, through a break in the walls of the tunnel? I remembered Mrs Tregenna telling me that some of the shafts ran right under the sea.

Why did Daniel have to risk his own life? But that was Daniel, wasn't it? A man filled with concern for others, a man who, fully aware of what could happen to him down there, still needed to help. Tom meant nothing to him. Daniel didn't even like him, and yet he was prepared to risk his own life to try to save him.

I remembered the warmth of his hand holding mine, the taste of his lips when we kissed, the colours patterning his hair as we stood together in the chapel on St Michael's Mount. The movement of his fingers, brushing grass from his cheek. The way he walked, the sound of his voice when he said my name. How his smile tilted the corners of his mouth, the tired creases that lined his forehead, the rumpled collar of his sweatshirt.

How could I exist without him?

I never saw the baby I lost. Never held it in my arms or kissed it. Never even knew whether it would have been a boy or girl. But I grieved for it, wept for it and dreamed about it over the years.

I simply couldn't bear to feel such loss again.

'Lissa!'

The crewman's voice jerked me alert.

'They're bringing them up.'

My teeth bit into my lip and I tasted blood. My fingers knotting together. My whole body shaking.

First came a stretcher carrying Tom, swathed in a foil blanket.

'Lissa!' His voice was a croaking whisper. 'Make sure they don't lose that film. It'll be fantastic!'

How typical of Tom to think of that first, I thought bitterly.

Moments later, Phil the camera-man appeared, supported either side by two paramedics.

'Hi, guys,' he murmured as he hobbled past. 'Don't worry, I just kept filming. It's all there. Roof fall, rescue, everything. It should be great.' Even in a situation like this, Phil was still a professional.

But where was Daniel? Why wasn't he with them? My mouth went dry. The young actor, the extras and crewman said goodbye and walked slowly outside to the waiting ambulances. I noticed a third vehicle still waited. With sirens wailing, the other two drove away.

Something had happened to Daniel. He should have come up by now. The room around me was empty. Silence surrounded me. Surely someone must realise he was still down there? Panic tensed my whole body. Blood pounded in my ears. I was fighting to breathe.

Footsteps echoed. I moved across the room, my heart thumping.

One of the fire-fighters trudged in, tugging off his helmet to wipe his face. 'Daniel,' I said, my voice shaking. 'What's happened to him?'

The man's teeth showed white as he grinned. 'Daniel's fine. He said to tell you he'll be up in a while. He's helping to clear some of the rubble, that's all. Whoops, Miss, now don't you go all faint on me.'

I was sitting, still shaking, trying to drink a mug of scalding tea that Jack, the guide, had provided, when Daniel appeared, soaking wet, his clothes torn and covered in dirt.

But it didn't matter. I was across the room and into his arms, tears streaming down my face.

'Oh, Daniel Tregenna, don't you ever, ever, do anything like that again.'

CHAPTER TEN

Daniel spoke slowly and softly, as we drove back through the winding lanes. 'Lissa, you never talk about your family. And with the wedding . . .'

My back stiffened. 'I don't have a family,' I retorted.

He frowned. 'But you must have. Everybody has a family. Come on now, Lissa. No more secrets.'

I looked out through the car window, seeing the soft colour of wild flowers covering the high grass banks and arched branches making a leafy tunnel above us, remembering. There was so much of my past life that I didn't want to remember.

The car stopped at a crossroads, then moved on again, and the waiting silence between us grew. No more secrets.

'My mother died when I was sixteen, Daniel. She'd been fighting leukaemia for several years. I was taking my last GCSE exam that day—English Literature.' I choked back the rising tightness in my throat. 'She died early in the morning. I should have been with her, Daniel, but no one told me what had happened until after the exam was finished.'

He reached across and squeezed my fingers.

'Lissa, darling, don't go on if it's too painful for you.'

'No, I need to tell you, Daniel. If we're to be married, you must know everything about me.' I shrugged. 'Even though afterwards, you may not want to marry me.'

'That will never happen, Lissa. I want you far too much.'

A grey squirrel hesitated in the long grass by the side of the lane, before scuffling across. Daniel slowed the car, then changed through the gears and speeded up again.

'I was devastated after she died. I'd always

refused to believe that it was going to happen. When she went into the hospice, I should have realised, but she was so very brave, never revealing to me just how bad things were. And I was too naïve to understand.'

'Do you have any brothers or sisters?'

'No, there's just me.'

'And your father?'

I clenched my teeth over my lower lip. 'Oh, yes, my father,' I said, unable to prevent the bitterness in my tone. 'I adored him. He was always there for me, all through my childhood. My mother was often in a wheelchair, but had bouts of remission when she seemed perfectly well. We even had the most fantastic holidays all together in a cottage in North Devon.' Memories were flooding into my mind. Memories of happiness, and I smiled. 'My father was a keen sportsman. He should have had a son. Instead, he taught me to sail when I was only eight, and hired a boat down there each summer.'

Closing my eyes, I could see him, hauling on the ropes as the yacht leaned perilously sideways, and I sat, drenched in spray, laughing with him. I could remember his laughter so well.

'When I was older, we learned to wind-surf together. All the bruises and aching limbs never worried him. And he was always there, ready to help me upright again, when a gust of wind tipped my board over.'

'When did he die?'

Daniel's words jolted through me. 'He's not dead,' I said abruptly.

'Then he'll come to our wedding?'

'No way!' I retorted. 'I thought my father would be devastated after my mother died. I was. Our whole life was shattered. Never to be the same.'

'Maybe he kept his feelings well hidden, Lissa, not wanting to upset you further. You were at such a vulnerable age at sixteen.'

Angrily, I shook my head. 'Within six months, he'd married again. My mother's sister. Can you credit that?' I leaned my head against the back of the seat, staring up at the roof of the car. 'She'd always been there. Living in the same town. Coming to look after me during those times when my mother's leukaemia was bad.'

We were approaching the gates of the house now, the Range Rover turning into the long driveway bordered by the pink, mauve and bright red flowers of rhododendrons.

'She was the one who wouldn't let them tell me my mother was dying, until after I'd taken my final exam. I hate her for that.'

'Oh, Lissa, darling.' Daniel stopped the car outside the house and gently kissed the top of my head.

'When my father announced he was marrying her, I left home. I haven't spoken to or seen him since that day.'

108

'But that's terrible, Lissa. All these years. Surely, by now, you can forgive and forget? You loved him so much, once, didn't you?'

'How can I? He destroyed that love and trust when he married her,' I replied, jumping down from the Range Rover.

'Hate is a vicious thing, Lissa. It eats into you.' He smiled ruefully. 'And men frequently do remarry quickly, after being widowed. We're not very good at coping alone.'

Mrs Tregenna was in the hallway, studying an envelope in her hand, when we went indoors. 'It looks very official, Daniel. I'm so intrigued.' Slitting it open, Daniel unfolded a letter, then raised one eyebrow.

'Well, at least this is good news,' he said. 'We've been granted the licence to hold weddings here.' He leaned across to kiss me and continued, 'Let's make ours the first wedding to be held here, shall we, Lissa?'

'Oh, my darlings!' The old lady clapped her hands like an excited child. 'That will be wonderful. When shall it be? Soon, please.'

After a couple of days, checking all future bookings for the hotel, we finally decided on a Wednesday, at the end of June. Mid-week, there would be no comings and goings of guests. Mrs Tregenna insisted on making all the arrangements.

'I never had a daughter, Lissa, and over these past months, you have become very dear to me.' From the depths of her armchair, she looked appealingly up at me. 'Please say you'll indulge an old lady.'

How could I refuse? 'Are you sure it won't be too much for you?' I asked anxiously. After all, she was in her eighties and quite fragile.

'Of course not, my dear. It'll give me a new lease of life. I love social occasions and we haven't had anything special here since the official hotel opening, have we?' She beamed back at me. 'Do you think your Wardrobe Department would loan me one of their magnificent hats again?'

I laughed, but at the back of my mind I was wondering whether I should invite those I'd worked with for so many years. They were my friends, and I had no family. But if I did, how could I exclude Tom?

'Look, Gran, it's going to be a quiet wedding,' Daniel warned, his expression worried. 'We don't want the whole Duchy of Cornwall turning up. If I had my way, it would be just Lissa and me—and you, of course.'

'Daniel, darling! This is us. The Tregennas.' She squeezed her thin shoulders together and chuckled. 'It'll be just like it used to be here. A really grand occasion.'

Daniel looked across at me and shrugged helplessly.

*   *   *

Tom's Cornish series was to be shown every

Sunday throughout June and the beginning of July. On the first evening, Daniel, his grandmother and I settled ourselves in front of television, after dinner, and waited as a panoramic scene very slowly panned across the screen.

'Oh, look!' Mrs Tregenna sat upright in her chair. 'Look! It's our driveway. And there's the house. Oh, darlings, doesn't it look spectacular?'

She peered more closely at the screen.

'Isn't that one of Mrs Tolly's sons? The young man, over there, scything the grass on the lawn. Oh, he's gone again.'

'Could be,' I said. 'Some of the locals were used as extras and he's a good-looking lad, isn't he?'

'I do hope Mrs Tolly is watching. She'll be delighted.'

'Maybe that'll find him a wife. She's always complaining about her sons lacking them,' Daniel teased. 'Wow! You'd never know that old staircase had been so dilapidated, would you? Paul Madron's done a brilliant job restoring it. Really sets off those beautiful dresses as the ladies come down, doesn't it?' Daniel commented, as the scenes continued. 'I have to admit that Tom is good, Lissa. It's a great production.'

'Well, he is one of the best—at directing,' I added. 'Doesn't change his character, though.'

Daniel's arm slid round my waist, hugging

111

me, and I happily nuzzled my cheek against his.

It was a good production. I knew it would be with Tom's direction, Peter's scripts and those clever actors who made the characters so real. And the Cornish countryside, with its old mine chimneys and engine-houses, bleak against the blue sky. It couldn't fail to be good.

'Oh, Lissa, look! It's your name. Oh, and there's the name of this house,' Mrs Tregenna shrieked excitedly. 'Look! Just moving up the screen. I do wish they'd go more slowly. How can anyone read it at that speed?'

I'd insisted that the name of the house appeared in the credits at the end of each episode. It wasn't just Tom who believed in good publicity! If the country house hotel was to succeed, in these times of recession, it needed all possible encouragement.

The following morning, I flicked through every newspaper to read the reviews and I wasn't disappointed. They were fabulous! Not one bad criticism. The comparison with the Poldark series was briefly commented upon, but only how different the two stories were.

For the rest of the week, the hotel telephone rang constantly with people eager to stay 'where that telly programme is filmed'. Local guest houses and B&Bs reported the same.

A week or so later I was sifting on a smooth rock by the edge of the shore, watching thin strands of seaweed swirl in and out with the waves, when my mobile shrilled, and I read who was calling. Tom. Reluctantly, I pressed the key.

'Lissa!' That familiar voice hadn't lost its abruptness.

'Yes,' I replied cautiously.

'Second series is in the bag. Need the house, okay? Peter will be there tomorrow—he has to check those diaries. I'll follow on.'

Before I could say a word, the phone went dead. Typical! I thought. When Tom says jump, you jump.

Not any more though. No longer did I work for him, or the company. But this was where the series had to be made, I accepted that.

Getting up, I hurried back to the house. Daniel had to know. And I dreaded his reaction.

'But he can't, Lissa. The hotel is far too busy,' Daniel replied, just as I'd expected. 'We can't have all that disruption here for weeks on end. Why can't he wait until the autumn, when everything slows down again?'

'Television doesn't work like that, Daniel. To be given a second series is amazing. And it does have to be now, to fit in with the right season of year.' I pushed back a strand of hair that had fallen over my eyes. 'A lot of the guests have only come to stay because of the programme. If they can actually watch it being made, that'll be an added bonus for them. I'm

113

sure they won't mind all the upheaval. Please, Daniel.'

'And what about our wedding, Lissa? Will Tom decide to disrupt that, too? Is that his real purpose?'

It was something that had crossed my mind as well, but I wasn't going to say so. Daniel disliked Tom, that I knew, and he had good reason.

'It's only the script-writer, Peter, coming tomorrow, Daniel. Maybe I can delay Tom until after the wedding.'

It was a vain hope, but I could try.

'Can't be done,' he barked, when I rang back. 'Deadlines to meet, Lissa. You should know what it's like.' His voice changed. 'Anyway, how about me giving you away at the wedding? Be quite fitting, wouldn't it? Handing you over for another man to enjoy.'

'No one will be giving me away,' I snapped. 'Least of all, you.'

*   *   *

Peter arrived and settled himself quietly in the library, to delve into Elizabeth Tregenna's diaries. Mrs Tolly was delighted to see him back and carried in hourly trays of tea, as if she feared his inspiration would suddenly dry up without them.

With only two days until the wedding, I was beginning to feel nervous. Why, I don't know. I

114

had no worries that Daniel loved me as deeply as I loved him. He left me in no doubt of that.

Everything was planned. My friends in the Wardrobe Department had insisted they make my dress and it was breathtaking. A slender sheath of white silk, falling in soft cowled folds at the neck and sweeping into a long train at the back. Nothing could possibly go wrong. Even the arrival of Tom wouldn't spoil it.

I was arranging a vase of delphiniums in Reception, when the desk phone rang and I answered it.

'Can I speak to Melissa Thornton?' a woman's faint voice enquired.

'Speaking,' I replied.

'Melissa!' There was a pause before the voice continued, hesitantly. 'It's your father, dear. I'm sorry to tell you he's had a massive stroke. I thought you should know. We saw your name in the TV credits the other Sunday. That's how I found you.'

For a moment, I had to take in deep, ragged breaths. This must be his wife, my aunt. The woman who'd destroyed my life all those years ago. My voice shook when I answered her. 'So why are you telling me?'

'You're his daughter, Melissa.'

She went on to name the London hospital, where he was in intensive care. Mechanically, I picked up a pen and wrote it down.

'Please, Melissa. For his sake, try to forget the past. We're all to blame. Just come, before

115

it's too late.'

Silently, I replaced the receiver.

'Darling, you have to go.' Daniel was quite firm, when I told him. 'I'll drive you up there. There won't be a through train until later today.'

'I'll drive myself, Daniel.'

'Let me be with you, Lissa.'

'I said, I'll drive myself.'

Reluctantly, he agreed, and within an hour I was on the A30, negotiating the heavy traffic, remembering my last frantic journey to the London offices, way back in the winter. That had been at night, when all the roads were clear, not clogged up with lines of huge lorries, driving row behind row, and holidaymakers ambling along.

Why am I doing this, I asked myself? Why should I care what happens to my father? He's never bothered about me for all these years.

But I was the one who walked out that day. The day that he told me he was to marry again. I was the one who refused to answer his phone calls, or letters. I was the one who'd created a barrier, hadn't I? Letting my hatred grow until it became impossible to apologise.

What had life been like for my father, with a wife permanently ill, confined to a wheelchair most of the time? He was still young. And my aunt had always been there, for both of us, when we needed her.

Maybe she was trying to be kind, not telling

116

me my mother had died, letting me finish my exam, knowing how I'd feel. Knowing how important those exams were for me. Knowing her own heartbreak at the death of her beloved sister. I'd never thought about that. Both she and my father had lost someone very close to them. Maybe that's why they had turned to each other for comfort.

And now? She was giving me the chance, this time, to be there, at the end. Would I be too late?

I thumped my hand hard on the horn, letting it blare in protest as a huge lorry raced out from the inside lane and slowed in front of me.

The slip road to the motorway appeared and I steered the car onto it to meet even heavier traffic. Sun blazed in through the windscreen. The temperature in the car was rising, even with the air conditioning.

Daniel had printed out the route from the Internet and stuck it to the dashboard. I glanced at it every so often when the road became unfamiliar.

Mrs Tolly had provided sandwiches and a flask of iced water, but if I pulled off the main road to stop, I'd never get back into the stream of traffic again, and it would all take time. Time, both I, and my father, didn't have.

At a roundabout, I took the wrong exit, travelling several miles before I could turn and go back to it. Why didn't I let Daniel drive me,

117

I thought? Why did I have to be so pig-headed?

My mouth was dry, desperate for water. My head ached from the blinding sunlight. My arms and hands were stiff, tensely gripping the steering wheel and my tee-shirt clung damply to my back. I wriggled my shoulders, trying to ease them, feeling the seatbelt cut across my chest.

Vehicles were nose to tail, hardly moving. Ignoring the blaring car horns, I turned when I saw the hospital entrance on the opposite side.

There had to be a parking space. As a green car moved backwards a few metres ahead, my foot stamped on the accelerator, and I shot forward into the gap, just before a small van reached it. With the driver's anger ringing in my ears, I ran to the main doors and through to Reception.

'David Thornton.' I managed to gasp. 'I'm his daughter.'

A lift winged me upwards, its doors whispered open and closed. On the sixth floor, I stepped out, footsteps echoing along the corridor. A nurse met me, handing me a plastic apron, making me wash my hands with something sterile, before she took me in.

The man lying there, tubes and wires snaking from his thin body, didn't look like anyone I recognised. My father was a tall man, a strong man. I remembered his laughter, the way his hands held the ropes controlling the sails on our boat, the smell of his aftershave when he cuddled me onto his lap, reading me stories before I went to sleep each night. Tears gathered behind my eyes, ready to brim over and scald my cheeks.

A woman was sitting by his bed, her fingers clasped round his, stroking his wrist. Pale face, lipstick-smudged mouth, once-dark hair now streaked grey, crumpled blouse. An old woman, not the lively, vibrant one I'd known, creating games to play in the garden, away from the sickroom indoors.

'Melissa?' Her voice was a thin thread. 'Thank you for coming.'

She held out a trembling hand. I looked down at it, seeing the thin gold band encircling her third finger, and a tear slid down my cheek.

Wearily, she stood up, indicating the chair. 'Stay with him, Melissa. Talk to him. They say he will hear a voice.'

She walked to the door, turned to look back at me, still weeping, then was gone.

I sat in the chair, not knowing what to do. My father's mouth and nose were partly obscured by a faintly clouded mask, and I noticed his once-thick black hair had thinned. An old man lay there now.

Coloured lines quivered across a monitor by his bed. Numbers changed. My father's life was on that screen.

Leaning forward, I touched his fingers.

'Dad.' I whispered uncertainly. 'It's me, Dad. Lissa.'

Did his eyelids flicker, I wondered? Could he really hear me?

'I love you, Dad. I always did. You know that, don't you? I was young, cruel, I didn't think.' The words were rushing out now, like a river in torrent. 'I didn't understand that you had a life, too. That was selfish of me, Dad. I only thought of myself, my feelings, my life, no one else.'

My tears would hold back no longer. They burned my skin, soaking into the thin blanket covering him. 'Forgive me, Dad. Please forgive me.'

Gently, I kissed his cheek, letting my own remain there for one long second, needing his comfort. Under my hand, his fingers seemed to quiver slightly. Or maybe I just wished they did. I heard his breath sigh out.

I don't know how long I sat there. The coloured lines on the monitor had stopped moving, and I knew I would never hear his laughter again.

The corridor stretched emptily in front of me, as I walked back to the lift. Someone rose from a chair by the window.

'Daniel,' I murmured, and was lost in his arms and his kiss.

'I've come to take you home, my darling.'

I discovered later that Daniel had brought Peter with him. While I travelled home in the

Range Rover, Peter drove back in my car that evening, bringing some of my TV friends with him.

'We'll postpone the wedding until later, Lissa,' Daniel said. 'Let you recover from all this.'

'No, Daniel! It's tomorrow. We can't spoil it for everyone. Especially your grandmother. She's spent so long, making sure everything will be so special. We can't disappoint her.'

'Gran will understand, my love.'

'No, Daniel,' I replied, quite firmly.

* * *

It couldn't have been a more beautiful day. A typically Cornish morning, blue sky, with a scattering of tiny white clouds, warm June sunshine, calm sea. And I knew I had to put aside my grief to make it perfect for everyone.

The setting for our wedding was the old wing of the house, in the lovely black and white tiled hall with its magnificent staircase.

Mrs Tregenna was at great pains to prevent Daniel and me from seeing each other before the ceremony. 'Bad luck,' she said, insisting I had breakfast in my bedroom and didn't appear downstairs until the allotted time of eleven o'clock.

With my dress, I was to wear a delicate white lace veil and a pale blue garter, both of which she'd worn, when married.

'Something old, something new, something borrowed, and something blue,' she said, with a chuckle. 'I think we can combine the borrowed and old bit, without it being too hazardous, don't you, my dear?'

I'd finally decided that Peter should give me away and he appeared, his freckled face broadly smiling, at the door of my room, promptly on time.

Together, we walked slowly down the curving staircase to where Daniel stood, his shaggy hair trimmed once again into some semblance of tidiness, immaculate in his dark suit. His expression was so full of love and wonderment that I thought my heart would break.

His grandmother outshone every other guest in her peacock silk dress and closely-fitted jacket, with a hat the Wardrobe Department had created specially for her. I was amazed her tiny body could support such a swathe of delicate flowers surrounding its straw brim.

The chef, instructed by Mrs Tolly, produced a banquet of food, with the centrepiece being one of Roskilly's ice-cream confections, lavish with meringue, clotted cream and strawberries.

Daniel and I were away on our honeymoon for most of the time that Tom and his crew took over the house for their filming. But with a third, and possibly fourth, series following the success of the other two, there's no way we can avoid being around in the future.

Peter says he has enough material from Elizabeth Tregenna's wonderful diaries to produce scripts for years to come, and our country house hotel becomes more popular and in demand with every re-showing.

Oh, I suppose you're wondering whether I ever saw that wistful child again, after Daniel and I were married. Well, I didn't. Not for many months, until last night that is. Then I woke, as I sometimes do now, and saw a tiny figure at the end of our bed. Not very tall, just a toddler. And yes, I know the room was dark, but I wasn't dreaming. I know for certain he was there, but this wasn't a sad-eyed little child.

This was James Daniel Tregenna, our own adorable little son.